THE VIEW FROM HAWKING'S BRIDGE

Donna Patrick

Cover photo by August Patrick

Donna Patrick
Visit my website at www.donnaknechtpatrick.wordpress.com

Printed in the United States of America

First Printing: July 2019

ISBN-978-1-7333051-0-5 (ebook)
978-1-7333051-1-2 (printed version)

Dedication

First, I need to thank Jim for sharing fifteen precious years of his life with me. Those years were an adventure to say the least; filled with joy, laughter, heartbreak and deep sadness, roses at stoplights and payments to the bail bondsman, The New York Times Sunday morning crosswords and lawn mower pulls in the back yard. Ours was a life full of contradiction, for better or worse. This book is dedicated not to you, but because of you, to those who struggle with life and to those who struggle to keep the ones they love alive.

I also need to thank Bernadette, my sister and friend. Always positive, never a complaint and an answer for every question I asked about the effects of M.S. on your life. You are a woman of indomitable spirit and a lifelong hero of mine.

Lastly, to my children, Anne, Stephan, Rebecca and August. You are my support and inspiration. I love each of you as the unique and awesome souls you are. Thank you for your love and encouragement.

Other Donna Patrick Books:

La Lune
What Celia Knows

CONTENTS

BLAME EDWARD

Prologue

1828

Elizabeth was melting. No parasol or feathered fan would be enough to save her from the glaring sun. She, her three month old boy and her beloved husband would die along this infernal road. *Oh, why couldn't Edward have considered her comfort for once and spent the extra money for a covered wagon?*

She saw her fair skin blistering before her eyes as her poor, sweet babe died in her arms, his throat too parched to let out a cry. Edward would stubbornly push on for as long as he could, taking his last breath while digging a grave for his family. Buzzards would pick their bones clean by the time they were found by another pioneering group, leaving little clue as to who the young Hawking family were in their tragically short lives.

She wondered why she had agreed to leave the safety of her mother's home in Charleston to join Edward in this folly. And to what end? A life of hardship and gnarled hands, that was certain. If she did survive the journey she could look forward to years of digging dirt while battling insects and rodents and Indians and possibly even mountain lions! Hacking at trees and mixing mud to build a home for their family was not the dream of most girls she knew.

Just as Mother warned, Elizabeth would now suffer for her constant refusal to train in Cotillion. Instead of teas and picnics there would be planting and harvesting, canning and sewing, all the drudgery of raising a family alone. There had been two choices for her to make as a young woman in Charleston society – a secure life in a loveless, boring marriage, or an adventurous life with a pioneering man like her Edward.

She loved Edward Hawking with all her heart and would walk with him through hellfire if he needed her to. She told him just that on the day he asked for her hand in marriage, and she had meant it. If only she'd had the forethought to know he would take her promise so exactly. And so quickly.

Edward's obsession over land began even before they were married. He often spoke about taming the wild land so abundant in the west. As soon as the territory was signed over by the Cherokee, Edward raced to the Ozarks and bought a thousand acres near the Arkansas/Missouri border. He'd returned to Elizabeth with promises of beautiful rolling hills replete with eagles soaring overhead and a cool river for her ankles in summer. It was all he talked about after his return and she was happy to share in his enthusiasm, putting aside her fears of leaving all which was familiar. Now, with a newborn baby in her arms, she wondered if they shouldn't have waited until the fall. Or perhaps another year or two.

"Please, Edward, couldn't we stop in the next grove of trees and rest? Each breath feels like my last in this torturous heat."

Edward showed no pity. "But we've only just begun the day, Lizzie. The horses are fresh and well watered. If we don't use the day to our advantage, it will be weeks before we arrive at our new home. Would you rather we travelled at night when the darkness shields our enemies and any other dangers lying ahead of us?"

Elizabeth pouted. "Well, at least it would be cooler at night," she countered. Kept to herself, she thought, *this misery better well be worth it.*

TRAUMA REVISITED

1

T he vibration of the phone rattled the glass table. Jackson sighed. "I finally have a day off. Call somebody else," he said to the phone, thinking it was his boss. Then he noticed his mother's number displayed there.

"Hi Ma," he answered.

But it wasn't Ma. It was Boyd, the special needs brother his parents had adopted into their family years ago. It was odd for Boyd to initiate a phone call, causing Jackson some concern at the sound of his voice.

"You got to come home, Jackson, for real this time! Ma's sick. You got to come home. Got to!" Boyd's voice was frantic. Jackson imagined his brother's fists pressed into the hollows of his cheeks as he paced the floor in wide, heavy steps.

"Where is she?" Jackson asked. "Let me talk to her." He wanted to make sure Boyd wasn't exaggerating the situation as he so often did.

"She's sleeping, Jackson. I told you, she's sick."

"But its Saturday," Jackson returned, shocked at the thought of his mother asleep on a Saturday afternoon.

"She sleeps all the time now. She's sick. Come home, Jackson!"

He'd never known his mother to lie down even when she was sick. Not even after a day's work at the mill. Not even after... Dad.

That was all he needed to confirm Boyd's panic. Something had to be wrong. "I'll be there tomorrow."

"Can't you come now?" asked Boyd.

Jackson looked around, considered what he needed to do to free himself from this place he'd settled into. There was nothing here for him and he had no intention of returning. "It will take me a minute to get there, Boyd. Be patient. You'll have to take care of Ma till tomorrow. Can you handle that?" Jackson could almost hear Boyd nodding at the phone. "Boyd?"

"Okay," he mumbled, disappointment in his voice.

The thought of Boyd being responsible for a sick Ma only served to remind Jackson of what a dick he'd been for leaving them in the first place. What had he been thinking? Boyd wasn't capable of taking care of Ma. She was his caretaker. Leaving them in the fallout of his father's death three years ago had seemed the only option for Jackson at the time. There was so much he regretted and so much he needed to apologize for. He'd stayed away because he wasn't near ready to face it. Now he had no choice.

The long drive gave him time to worry not only about his mother's health, but that of his own. A knot formed in his stomach and grew as each mile passed, until it encircled his heart and began the familiar squeeze. Every bend in the road forebode his doom. Every hill crest increased his anxiety. He knew every inch of this ground, had scoured the land as a kid; driven the roads as an adult. What once meant home and safety now threatened his very being. All the Tums in the world couldn't touch the burning sensation making its way to his throat as he took the last turn and approached the inevitable *goddamned bridge*.

A heart attack was looming, he just knew it.

"Damn this place, and damn you for making me feel like this!" With a few deep breaths he tried to overcome the squeezing, without success. He felt the tires slip into the grooves of the wooden deck. The iron trusses above seemed to swallow him up as he pushed forward, the rails at his sides threatening to close in.

Hurrying across the bridge and up the bluff, he slammed the truck into Park and rested his head against the steering wheel as soon as he was in front of the house.

C'mon, one breath at a time. That's all it is. In...and out...

The screen door slammed. Boyd's shuffling feet scoured the ground outside the truck. When Jackson lifted his head, he knew Boyd's face would be pressed against the window. He could hear the repressed chuckle and see the big toothed grin even before he turned toward it.

Yep. There it is.

"Hey, Boyd," he said, straightening himself up and pulling in one last long breath. He forced a smile.

Boyd was on him the moment he left the cab, hugging Jackson with all his might. Every time he seemed to let up and Jackson thought he was free, the squeezing began again. By the fourth time, Jackson had to chuckle to himself. If he was having a heart attack, at least he was getting compressions. For all he knew, Boyd might even be saving his life.

"You act like you missed me or something," he said with a cough.

Boyd nodded into Jackson's chest.

"Ever day."

Smiling eyes looked up at him.

"Ever day I said my prayers and asked Jesus to make you come home. And you know what? It worked."

Jackson couldn't blame Boyd for feeling lonely. The poor guy had gotten caught in a fustercluck he had no control over or blame for.

None of it had been his fault. In fact, Boyd had been Jackson's only reason for staying in the days after their father's death. Everyone else but Boyd had unnerved him to no end.

"How's Ma?"

Boyd shrugged. "Same. Still sleeping."

Still? It wasn't even dark yet.

"Let's go see."

Jackson grabbed his bag and followed Boyd into the house, making sure not to look back behind them, toward the mill, or the bridge he just crossed. The Hawking family legacy was a heavy load he didn't feel prepared to carry just yet.

Before Boyd could run ahead and announce his arrival, Jackson pulled him aside and asked him to put on a pot of coffee. It was a task he had taught his younger brother before anyone else trusted Boyd enough to go near the stove, never mind turn it on. Jackson thought running some water and filling the basket with coffee grounds was well within his abilities. At ten years of age, it had been long past time for Boyd to start taking on some chores around the house, but their parents had been too overprotective to consider it.

Jackson peeked in to his mother's bedroom before entering. She lay under a blanket on top of her bedspread, her back to the door.

His first step caused a floorboard to creak. She stirred. He stopped, not wanting to wake her, but she turned and faced him. Silence filled the room as she looked closer.

"Jackson? What? What are you doing here, honey?" Her voice was thick with sleep.

"Don't get up, Ma, I didn't mean to wake you."

"I told him not to call you." She slowly sat upright, fixing her hair and adjusting her clothes.

Jackson approached her. "Ma, don't. He didn't. Just lie back down. You don't have to get up for me."

"Well, of course I do. My boy is home. He needs a hug. Come here," she said as she reached out for him. "Are you home to stay?"

He sat down next to her and allowed her thin arms to enfold him.

"I'm home to make sure you're okay," he said, his eye going to the device standing between the bed and side table. A box of syringes sat next to the lamp.

"You're using a cane?" He asked it too sharply.

She pulled back, sighed and nodded.

"For a while now. Isn't it pretty, though? I picked out a purple one this time. The first one was always falling over. This one stands on its own."

"This time? Ma, how long have you needed a cane to walk? And what is all this about?" He pointed to the syringes.

"That's for my medicine." She said it like it was no big deal.

"What medicine?"

"I get a shot every day."

He shook his head, bewildered. "Shots? Why is this the first I'm hearing of any of this?"

She waved him off.

"I don't want to talk about that right now, I'm tired of it all. I want to talk about you." She looked him over. "How are you? How amazing are all the caverns of the world?"

He shook his head again, this time in disregard. "They're all dark, Ma. None of that matters now. I'm worried about you."

You have a funny way of showing it, being gone for three years, dick.

Trying to push the guilt from his head, he apologized.

"I'm sorry, Ma. I'm sorry I've been gone for so long. I should have done a better job of checking in on you and Boyd all this time. Phone calls aren't enough. I'm sorry I haven't been here to visit."

She gave him a weak smile. "You're here now, aren't you? That makes me happy. You can stay home for a while?"

She wanted reassurance, but how could he answer such a question? He felt so lost, he wasn't even sure he was home.

"Coffee's ready," Boyd said from the doorway. "I made it extra special." His grin showed how proud he was.

"Yeah?" Jackson was glad for the interruption. "What extra special ingredient did you use this time?"

Boyd giggled, "You'll see," before shuffling back to the kitchen.

"I hope it's not one of his cayenne pepper concoctions," Ma complained.

Jackson turned and noticed Ma struggling to reach her cane while shimmying off the bed.

"Let me help you." Jumping up and grabbing her arm, he noticed how fragile she'd become and released some pressure.

What the hell was going on here?

He supported her as she held the cane and pulled herself to stand. Then she took one step with her right foot, planted the cane and dragged her left foot up to it.

Never had he seen his mother so vulnerable, so weak. She may have been small in stature, but in his mind, she had always been mighty. At 5'2", she was the only one Jackson had ever known to be able to stand up to the towering Trevor Hawking.

As soon as she got her bearings she shook Jackson's arm free.

"You can let go of me now," she said, and the woman he had always known was back.

THOSE AWFUL M'S

2

*C*innamon, *thank God*, thought Jackson as he took his first sip of coffee. In between continued hugs from his adopted brother, he stole glances around the room.

The house was different somehow. Although the photos of Nana and Papaw flanking Uncle Paul hung in their usual places, they were tilted off-square with the wall. A layer of dust had accumulated on the shelves where Ma's Painted Ponies collection ran free. These were two things which would have driven her to distraction a few years ago, but she seemed not to notice now.

Her hand trembled as she pulled the cup to her lips.

Jackson couldn't take the suspense any longer. "So, tell me what's going on with you. We can't sit here and act like nothing's wrong."

"She's got the M's," said Boyd.

"MS," his mother corrected. "Multiple Sclerosis. He knows what it is, he just thinks he's being funny." She said it directly to Boyd, letting him know she was on to him. Then she turned back to Jackson. "Remember all those times my sciatica acted up and I'd hobble around for a few days? Well, it wasn't sciatica like the doctors thought. That was just the beginning of it. That, and the times when my hands would tingle or my legs would ache for no reason. It was all those little things I put off as me getting older or being tired from a long day. I didn't know any better and we never put the pieces together. They finally diagnosed me in November after my hands got so weak I started dropping things."

"She broke my cup," Boyd accused her. "Elvis."

Ma very patiently leaned over and apologized to Boyd, probably for the millionth time, Jackson figured. Then she promised she would have Jackson order him a new one now that he was home.

"You say you were diagnosed in November?" he asked. "When did you start using a cane?"

"Around the same time, I guess."

Jackson's mind was whirring. "So, you went from dropping a few things to your foot dragging in what, five months? I didn't realize it could happen so fast. I thought MS was a long, drawn out sort of disease, like Lou Gehrig's or something."

"Jackson," said Boyd, vying for his brother's attention. "M. S." He said and then hid his face behind his coffee cup.

Jackson didn't take the bait and concentrated on his mother.

"Lou Gehrig's is not the same kind of disease," she answered. "And apparently MS is entirely different in different people. Some may never be diagnosed because their symptoms aren't severe enough. Some people are diagnosed and only ever have one or two symptoms for years and years. They might even feel better for a while and then it comes back, kind of like a roller coaster of good and bad for most of their lives. Then other people, people like me, well, we tend to progress in only one direction, and unfortunately, it's downward. At least that's what they tell me." She took a deep breath. "I'm sorry to say that for me, my best day will always be yesterday." She reached out and touched Jackson's worried face. "I'm sorry. I know it's not the best news. But it's the only news I've got."

He placed a hand over hers and looked at her, misty eyed.

"Emmm Essss," sang Boyd, still trying to get his brother's attention, to no avail.

"It's not fair. You've been through enough already." He swallowed to rid himself of the pain at the back of his throat. "I'm so sorry I left you alone to deal with this."

"Aww," she patted his shoulder, "you did what you had to do, son, I don't blame you for that. And I'm not alone. I have Boyd here to help me. And Natalie. They've both been a great help."

"Mmmm. Esssss," Boyd tried again.

"Natalie? What do you mean, Natalie's helping you?"

"Well, you know we always saw her as family, and after you left, she came to help with the mill. That young man you hired still works with Boyd in the granary, but Natalie works with me in the shop. She keeps the books and stocks the shelves. And who do you think gives me those shots? I needed the help Jackson. I'm sure you can understand how hard it's been with all of this doctor foolishness goin' on."

Jackson barely heard a word after Natalie's name was mentioned.

"She's working in the mill? Why is this the first I'm hearing about it? What's with all this secrecy? You don't tell me you're sick. You don't tell me about this... this arrangement you've made with my ex-girlfriend. It's not like we haven't talked, Ma. I have a cell phone. You know the number. What's up with that?"

This time Boyd chirped his brother's name. "Jackson. Look." He held the cup on top of his head and then unsuccessfully attempted to go hands free.

Jackson controlled the impulse to look, although he could see Boyd catch the cup from the corner of his eye, coffee spilling into his hair.

"What's up?" Ma stormed back at him. "Did I question your decision to leave everyone and everything behind after your father's death? No. I respected your choice. I knew you had your reasons, you didn't need to convince me what they were. The most important thing was, you felt justified in making that decision. Was I was hurt by it? Yes. But I forgave you."

The conversation between mother and son intensified as Boyd's plea for attention escalated. Boyd began saying his brother's name over and over, but not louder; more gently, in fact, as if he realized his interruption was going to be ignored, but his need for attention was unstoppable just the same.

"Jack. Son. Jackson. Jaaaaacccksoooonnn," he whispered as a ghost in a movie, exaggerating his lips to the point of his own distraction.

"Well maybe you shouldn't have let me off so fast. Maybe that's the problem, Ma, you forgive too easy. Just like you always forgave *him*. Like you did with all his drinking. Maybe if..." He stopped himself and shook his head.

Ma's face went red. "You think I'm going to play that game with you? The 'what if' I'd done something different, he'd still be alive? You think I haven't played it myself? You think I never asked him to stop drinking? Or begged him to stop? As if I had any control over what he did? You think I didn't do my best to make him happy?"

"Mmmmm. Sssssss. Emsss. Ems. See, Jackson? Ems. She's got the M's."

"By keeping him prisoner here?" Jackson blurted it out and then went quiet, knowing he'd gone too far. He never intended to unmask his anger toward his mother. "No, Ma, that's not what I meant... I'm sorry. Never mind. I didn't mean to upset you." He turned toward Boyd. "Not now, Buddy," he said, hoping he would stop, that it all would stop, *this whole conversation needs to stop.* He shifted in his chair, eyeing the door.

"No, no, no," said Ma, putting out her hand to pause the action he hadn't yet taken. "You want to lay blame? Now, let's see where we can lay blame." She began counting off on her fingers. "Let's see. I guess if I hadn't agreed to marry your father, he wouldn't have had a family to take care of and maybe he wouldn't have felt so stuck. So I guess that does makes me responsible. Or going back in time, maybe if Papaw hadn't expected him to take over the business after Uncle Paul died, your dad would have been spelunking around the world like he wanted to instead of meeting me." Testing his patience, she put a finger to her forehead, imitating the Scarecrow, mouth open, deep in thought. Her voice rang with sarcasm. "Or maybe it goes back further than that! Maybe if your ancestors had never built the mill in the first place, your dad wouldn't have been expected to run the family business which made him depressed and gave him the excuse to drink. And then maybe if the bridge had never been built, he wouldn't have jumped from it. And you know what else? Maybe if his failure to keep the mill turning a profit didn't weigh on him every single day... Did you know he was running the business into the ground? No, you probably didn't know that. On purpose, so he could be done with it once and for all," she said angrily, but then the anger turned raw and tears filled her eyes. "He struggled with it every day, Jackson. The guilt. The pressure. That's why he drank. He hated himself as much as he hated this place. He wanted out so badly, he was trying to kill himself along with the mill. I guess I should be thankful he only succeeded at the one."

There were no words to respond with. Even Boyd sat still.

"Okay," she said, dusting off her hands, "that's enough for me. I'm going back to bed." She used her cane to pull herself up and then stepped toward Jackson. "I love you, my son, and I'm very glad you're here. I'm just sorry there's so much we never got to hash out before you left. Maybe now we'll get that chance." Then she kissed his forehead before hobbling toward Boyd and doing the same. "Good night, boys."

Jackson watched until she closed her bedroom door, then got up from the table. He patted his brother's shoulder before walking out to the porch. Taking a seat at the top of the steps, he pulled in several long breaths to calm his anxiety. There seemed to be no relief.

Looming through the darkened trees, lighted by the rising moon, stood the arch of the infamous bridge, the metal structure his father chose as the instrument of his death. The place which held the most terrifying moments of Jackson's life.

All he wanted to do was push those memories away. Send them down river to the cool waters of the lake. There they would be diluted by all the other tragedies floating deep within it. Was it so wrong to want that?

"Take these images from me, Lord," he cried. "I don't want them in my head anymore."

A cool breeze picked up and stirred a memory of spelunking with his dad. They were exploring one of the lake's cooler caves on a hot summer day. It was one of the happier times of his life and for a moment the memory took away his pain.

His dad may never have gotten the chance to explore the Mulu caves of Malaysia, but he would often take the boys on local expeditions. The Ozarks had quite a bit to offer any cave enthusiast. Those trips had seemed like such fun to Jackson. The question was, when did the local stuff become "not enough" for his father? And, more importantly, when did his father's unrealized dream become his death sentence?

The screen door opened and then closed as Boyd shuffled toward Jackson, taking a seat beside him on the steps. They sat silent for a time, a surprising but welcome feat for Boyd to achieve.

"Thanks for being quiet with me, Buddy. I'm not really in the mood for talking right now."

"Natalie says sometimes there are no words."

"Yep, Natalie would say that," said Jackson. "She always knows the right thing to say. And the right thing to do."

Perfectly perfect Natalie, he thought. Of course she would have put aside her own feelings about him and stay around to help the mother and brother he abandoned. He should have expected no less. Now he would be forced to face her, much sooner than he ever expected to. *Oh boy.*

A HEFTY LEGACY

3

Natalie. It had been quite some time since Jackson allowed himself to dwell on her. He knew all too well where it would lead. More guilt, pangs of regret. But now, even as he tried to push them away, remembrances of a happier time snuck up on him like a copperhead in the grass. Like the times they spent racing their horses along the river, or jumping from the bluff into Escher's Creek. Long discarded dreams of a blissful future were forcing their way into his consciousness, dwelling there even when he screamed for them to get out. Happiness wasn't something he deserved or even sought.

There's no such thing as happiness. It's a myth. A lie men tell themselves to get through meaningless days.

There was a time when Natalie represented that myth, when he considered a life built around her and the mill as perfect bliss. What a fool he'd been to think their love would ever be enough, that surrendering to his family's legacy would somehow make his life complete.

Look what it had done to his father. Outwardly, Trevor Hawking had been a man hard at work for his family. He was a good neighbor, had friends; was devoted to his church. Everyone saw him as a good man, a man of strength and purpose, and for a long time he played the part well.

What they all missed, even Ma, was the gradual shift to his internal voice, where Trevor spent too much time alone with his thoughts. The place where his demons thrived.

Beneath the surface festered a man so trapped by destiny, his only escape was through a river of alcohol. The dangerous mix of resentment and drink propelled Trevor Hawking to destroy all the good in his life and eventually lead to his justification for ending it.

Jackson had no intention of ending up as angry and disappointed as his father. There was a time when he seemed headed down that same misguided path. At least until that fateful night when Trevor made Jackson's future so horrifically clear.

All evening Jackson had kept out of his father's way, avoiding the tirade he knew was coming. There was no avoiding the inevitable. Trevor caught him trying to escape across the bridge and pulled him into a conversation that would end life as he knew it.

"That girl," his father seethed, a half-empty bottle of whiskey held at his side. "She'll reel you in and make you believe you're the happiest asshole on the planet, and then you'll never be able to live up to what she expects. You'll fail at being a good husband, or father, or whatever everyone thinks a Hawking should be, no matter how hard you try. You'll be reminded of your failure every day, in every turn of that water wheel and grinding of that millstone. Every hope you have for a new adventure will be crushed under the weight of this goddamned family legacy and what she thinks it should mean."

If he'd known what was coming, Jackson would have agreed with the man, given him the benefit of the doubt just to satisfy him. But he couldn't have known the man was out of his mind.

"Your life will be nothing but heavy bags of grain and the constant threat of disaster. Eventually you'll resent the mill, the bridge leading to your home, and the woman who shares that home with you, same way I do. And just like me, you'll be powerless to stop it."

All the dreams Jackson had allowed himself to consider as a young man were being exposed as foolish. He felt impotent to stop it.

"You think there's something to be proud of in keeping this mill running? Starting over after every flood and every fire? Why? Because Papaw romanticized all those old family legends for you? I never should have let him get his hooks in you. He made you think life was going to be some glorious adventure. Do you know how many times that firetrap has been restored? Or how many times this bridge has been washed away and had to be rebuilt? Does that make sense to you? To get knocked down and keep getting up just to get knocked down again? What's the goddamn point?" He took a swig from the bottle. "Think about it. It's not like the mill has done anything great for us. Are we able to go on nice vacations or buy expensive things like other people do? Hell, no. Every day we break our backs and then once every few years we get to chase our supplies downstream in the flood waters, or put out the fire from a lightning strike. Idiocy. That's what it is. If you think this place is going to make you happy, or that *she's* going to make you happy, you're an idiot too." He slurred half the words, but seemed to have a clear grasp of what he wanted to say.

Jackson felt the need to bolt and run, but he knew it would be futile. Trevor would eventually catch up to him and then things might get physical. As fit as Jackson was, he was no match for his father. Even drunk.

"Your Papaw, you know, the guy you looked up to more than me? The one who told you if you worked hard and took care of the mill you'd get something in return? That it would give you a sense of purpose?" He threw the bottle to the side and placed his thumbs under his armpits, mocking his own father. 'Pride in a job well done', he'd say. 'Work is its own reward.' Somehow, the work made it all worth it, right?" He leaned in closer, breathing alcohol into Jackson's face. "Bullshit!" he spat. "It was all bullshit!"

Jackson knew his father was wrong. He argued every point being made, but only in his mind, growing angrier at each of his father's assertions that everything he knew was a lie and his ideas were all misguided. As far as Jackson was concerned, the only "bullshit" was coming from the drunk standing before him. Outwardly he listened with intent, but the voice in his head was screaming, *you are wrong, wrong, WRONG!*

He had certainly heard variations of this rant before, but on this night, there were two very distinct differences. First, it became a personal attack on Jackson, not just the usual rant about Papaw and his blind faith in the Hawking legacy. This time Trevor meant to demean and humiliate his own son. Second, it ended with Trevor jumping from the very bridge they stood on, into the dark, swollen river below. His body would be found just before sunrise, a half-mile downstream, wedged in a tangle of downed trees and waterlogged branches.

Jackson trudged through his father's funeral in a daze, hearing his words over and over as those last moments replayed in his head. Why would he have ended his life like that? It didn't make any sense.

Unless he'd been right about everything he'd said. He had to be right. He'd been right all along. He took his own life because no one could see how alone and trapped in this existence he was.

Throughout the funeral and after, Jackson listened to friends and neighbors judge his father's actions. Even Reverend Paulsen faulted Trevor for not putting his faith in God. With every assessment Jackson grew angrier. What right did they have to judge? They knew nothing of his father's burdens.

It was in those moments of enlightenment that Jackson decided his life would be different. He would listen to the words of his father and reject the Hawking legacy. He would discard it all as Trevor said he should, including Natalie. How stupid he'd been to think she was everything he needed. She would be the rock tied to his neck, pulling him further down into the river he wished more than ever to escape. Ridding himself of her was the first step away from a wasted life.

Once that was done, he was free to fulfill his father's dream.

WHERE'S A GOOD HIDEY-HOLE WHEN YOU NEED ONE?

4

His anxiety building with every step, Jackson forced himself to stand at the bluff overlooking the bridge and the mill beyond. He used to love standing there, thinking himself lord over all he surveyed. *Just a few more steps to the edge... A painful tumble to the bottom... Gulp water into your lungs... QUIT IT!!!* He reprimanded himself. *You are not your father!* All that time ago and the pain was still as fresh as yesterday. He shook out his arms to release the tension, then sucked in a deep breath of the cool morning air. *What is wrong with you?*

A car pulled into the parking lot near the mill. He bristled, somehow knowing it was "her". "Great," he muttered. Like it or not, he'd be pressed to face her. Already. Of all the conflicts he knew he'd be dealing with in returning home, this was one he thought he could put off for a while. Apparently not.

Be strong, he told himself. *She's going to try and disarm you with her forgiveness. Don't get sucked in to it. You don't deserve her forgiveness.*

Watching Boyd run across the gravel lot and holding on to her for dear life was confirmation of her presence. In a demonstration of mutiny, his own heart jumped, racing ahead to her even as he pulled himself back. He treated himself to a long, deep, cleansing-of-Natalie breath.

How many times had he thought of this moment? How many ways had he played out scenes of a chance meeting on the street, or at some gas station, or in a bar? He would let her know how quickly he'd moved on so she'd never be confused about his intentions.

"Has it been three years? Wow. Wish I had more time to catch up, but... Got to go." *It's that simple. Be on your way and don't look back. Don't start apologizing. She doesn't need to know what power she holds over you. Just calm, cool and distant. That's all she gets.*

As he made his way to the bridge, anxiety intensifying, nerves on fire, he watched her talking to Boyd. Just like the old days, she would keep his attention by getting right up in his face, constantly feeding him validation and love. And just as always, he was eating it up. How could he not? Even from fifty yards away Jackson could see she was still beautiful. It was impossible not to look at her. Not even the churning river below, the in-your-face reminder of his heartache and struggle, could distract him from the sight of her. Her long, dark-roast hair pulled up into a ponytail, allowing her face to brighten the day. Those deep, chocolatey eyes smiling...

"Jackson!" Boyd called. "Natalie's here! Look, its Natalie!" Boyd was doing his best impression of a pogo stick, his nervous energy jumping off the charts.

Jackson shook his head. Like a dog so excited for your return when all you did was go out and get the mail.

There was no getting around the awkwardness. No way of slipping by her and finding a good hidey hole in the mill. He could feel himself being inspected as he stepped across the rocky ground.

Show her nothing. Cool and simple, he told himself over and over.

As he got closer, close enough to look her in the eye, she gave him a smile. Instead of warming him the way it used to, it made him even more uncomfortable. He couldn't help it. His nerves were tighter than a bowstring pulled to launch.

Why is she here, anyway?

"Why are you here, Nat?" he asked.

The smile left her eyes. Clearly this wasn't the reaction she'd expected. She looked away and cleared her throat. "Well, hello to you too. No worries, Jackson," she explained in a soft voice. "I'm not here for you."

"Good thing." Jackson's response was not so soft. In fact, it was spit at her with a venom he really hadn't intended.

Natalie's head tilted, her face flushing with anger.

"Wow, no pleasantries? We're going to get right to it? Okay. Would you rather I stop working for your mother?" she asked.

She had no right to inject herself into his family after he'd broken things off. It only made him look even more like an asshole. Again Jackson surprised himself with his answer.

"Doesn't really matter to me, Natalie. It's your life. You fucking decide." The anger boiled out of him, unrestrained.

"Ooh, that's a cuss word! That's a quarter," Boyd demanded delightedly, holding out a trembling hand toward the offender.

Jackson turned, ready to pounce until he realized it wasn't Boyd he was angry with. Impatiently digging into his pockets, he pulled out some change and handed it over.

"Here, take it," he seethed, his eyes set again on Natalie's. "There's some extra there for whatever else you might hear."

"So this is how it's going to be?" Her voice, at once raspy and yet pixie-like, drew him in as it always had, threatening his resolve.

He managed to stay his ground. For the life of him, he couldn't understand why.

Shrugging his shoulders, he gave her a look of indifference. "I guess it is," he answered defiantly. "If you're looking for love and hugs, you'll have to talk to Boyd. I'm sure he'll accommodate you. He's always had a soft heart. Right Boyd?" Jackson tugged his brother's shirt.

"Lindsey made me a heart," Boyd answered, the sarcasm flying right by him.

"That's right, Boyd, you showed me last night," Jackson said. An exaggerated wink and a nudge from his elbow caused his brother to blush. "Lindsey's a very special girl."

Lindsey was Boyd's one true love; a feisty, fiery young woman with Down's syndrome he'd met in a sixth grade Special Ed class. They'd been two explosive peas in a pod ever since, even after their graduation from high school. Jackson had always thought she was precious and was glad to know Boyd maintained their friendship.

"Yep, she's Boyd's special girl, for sure." Natalie prodded Boyd playfully, attempting to change the conversation to something more agreeable.

Nice try.

As Boyd blushed again, saying something sweet about his girl, Jackson patted his shoulder, interrupting him. "Listen, I need to check on some stuff, see how the mill's doing. Now, don't forget the horses." He then turned to Natalie, who was clearly ruffled by his quick dismissal. "See ya." He waved her off and walked away.

And that was that. Or at least he thought it was. His plan was to escape into the recesses of the mill, put his mind to his work and forget about the last few minutes.

Natalie apparently had other plans.

THE DROWNER OF MEN

5

The best way to burn off nervous energy had always been loading sacks of grain on to the elevator, so that's what he set his mind to, whether it needed to be done or not. It wasn't long before he heard Natalie came up behind him, clearing her throat to get his attention.

"Jackson," she said softly.

His back stiffened at the sound of her voice, throwing him off balance. At first fighting to steady the large sack on his right shoulder, he then gave up, threw the sack down hard and wheeled around to face her.

"What, Natalie? What do you want from me?" he growled impatiently. "It's ridiculous to go over all this again. I don't feel any different than when I left."

Liar.

She looked into his soft grey eyes, perhaps hoping for a glimmer of what she used to love about them.

"I-I just wanted a chance to talk to you," she said, hands clasped together. "I know how awkward this is. I thought maybe we could come to some sort of agreement on how to handle it."

"Oh, you think this is awkward?" He chuckled. "I'm gone for three years and I come back to find the girl I broke up with working in my mill? Alongside my family? No, nothing awkward about that."

"You think I'm doing it to get back together with you, is that it? To stay in your family's good graces? Or to get back *at* you in some way? I'm not here to make you feel guilty for leaving. Have you ever considered this has nothing to do with you at all?"

He hadn't, as a matter of fact.

She went on even though he wished she'd just go away.

"I never blamed you for your decision to leave, Jackson, and neither did your mother. Whatever your father said to you that night made you feel you had to distance yourself, even from me. I get that. I certainly didn't agree with your choice and it broke my heart, but you had to do what was best for you. So, okay, we all let you go. Even Boyd. He resolved to leave you be and put his heart and soul into taking over for you. I think you'll be able to see how much he's grown since you've been gone."

He had noticed some maturity in Boyd, but he wasn't about to add to the conversation. *That's how she pulls you in.*

"I just want you to know why I'm here, Jackson, why I choose to return every day to the place that, in all honesty, should be the last place I'd want to be. This place holds all the hopes I had for a future with you and all the memories we shared, good and bad." Looking down, she began to pull at the hem of her shirt, something Jackson remembered her doing whenever she was unsure of herself. "My mom thinks I'm crazy for coming back here. She thinks I have no self-respect. My friends think I'm a glutton for punishment. That's because they all think what you did was unforgivable." She looked up at him, her brown eyes glistening with remembrance. "But they're wrong, I know they are, and the only other person who understands that is your mother. I come here because she's the only person I can talk to about the heartache you left me with. I can't talk to them about that stuff because they already hate you and that's not what I want. I'm tired of them trashing you. They're supposed to have compassion and understanding, but they don't. I know they're only trying to be protective – but I don't need their protection, I just need them to listen and they can't seem to do that without pushing their hateful opinions on me. Ma just isn't like that."

Jackson stood motionless, his eyes following the line of the woman before him. Her face had changed since the last time he'd seen her, her eyes just a little sharper, along with her jawline. The roundness of her youth had settled into a new body, full and curved in all the right places. Some would say too full. Papaw would have called her "sturdy". Jackson saw her as a beautiful woman, with warm eyes silently pleading. For what? Reconciliation? Acknowledgement of a love which had never died?

"My mother's always been a good listener," he said. "She looks past the things other people get stuck on. She's never been one to hold a grudge."

"I know. That's what I'm saying. She's awesome, isn't she?"

He wanted to walk away, to end it there and go about his business, but he couldn't. Natalie wasn't just anyone. He couldn't ignore what was standing right in front of him. He couldn't discard the truth. He nodded. "She's just like you."

Without a thought he took a step toward her and touched her hair, searching her dark eyes. They were fixed on him. No quiver, no falter, no questioning herself. An overwhelming urge drew him closer. His hands cupped her face, then his lips touched hers and he felt her take a breath; that startled gasp of excitement he also felt within himself. He gave in to the will of his body and engulfed her in his arms the way he once had. It was impossible not to.

It was as if they'd never left each other's embrace, in fact, had always been standing there entwined in this passion fueled by a touch. So much about her was the same. Her full frame melting into his, so easy to enfold. Her kiss was as it had always been, tender and yielding and then provoking and powerful. He felt himself letting go, allowing his mind to float back to the familiar. To the days spent walking in the meadow or lying under the mimosa tree where they first discovered one another. To the whispers of intent and soft giggles in the dark; all reminders of the love they once shared. The warmth of remembrance soothed him... until glimpses of less happy memories began to make their way into his unsuspecting brain.

Suddenly he was standing on the bridge, his father accusing Natalie of being the weight meant to anchor him there. First acknowledging the love and passion which had brought Jackson and Natalie together, then explaining how, given time, the growing resentment would cause a great rift between them. The distance would become wider with each inevitable struggle, he said. "Yes," his father admitted, "she's pretty and bright, but too wise and sympathetic for you. Instead of criticism, each failure of yours will bring kind words of understanding from her. And trust me, there will be failures." He made clear how Natalie's kindnesses would only emphasize the depth of Jackson's imperfections. As she grew in her benevolence from these acts of forgiveness, his weaknesses would be grudgingly revealed. "In the end, you'll realize you never deserved her or her generosity to begin with. You'll be drowning in regret."

Jackson's mind pulled him harder into the torturous words of his father, as if every thought of Natalie brought out the remembrance of the last few moments spent with him, his feelings for her so woven into the fabric of his father's death that he seemed unable to separate them. There was no controlling it. He began to feel sick, and not just in the emotional sense.

Nausea welled up inside him, cold bumps suddenly rising from his clammy, disobedient skin. Panic overtook him as he desperately tried to tamp it down and failed. He broke from the kiss and ran off toward the nearest exit. There was no time to make excuses or apologies.

Desperately trying to reach the unforgiving river ahead, he lost the fight, his breakfast, and whatever was left of his imagined manhood in the dirt along its banks.

PRAYING FOR WALNUTS

6

That night, at dinner with Ma and Boyd, the awkwardness continued.

"I hear you had some sort of run-in with Natalie this morning," said Ma, annoyance in her voice. "Did you really think it necessary to -,"

Jackson interrupted his mother with the defensive. "What did she tell you? That I was the biggest asshole on the planet?"

As Boyd held out his hand asking for another quarter, his mother sat back in surprise.

"Actually, Natalie hasn't said a word to me about you. It was Boyd who showed me the change you gave him for his jar. Now I can see why," she said with a righteous tone.

Jackson felt like an idiot. The use of profanity in his mother's house had always been strictly managed, even when his father was in full-on-drunk mode. Hence the quarter per cuss rule. Before Boyd was old enough, Jackson was the cuss-jar keeper. On days when his dad's friends came over to drink and play cards, he made out like a bandit. *The Cuss Bandit*, they called him. It didn't matter if they were playing at a table over in the mill, out of earshot of Ma. Young Jackson was glad to enforce the rules in any arena.

"Sorry, Ma," he said quietly. "It's been a rough day."

"Rough?" She then took a feeble hand and ran it the length of her body, like a shaky model showing off her designer duds. "Do you think I don't know what a rough day is like?"

"No, Ma, I know-"

"Do you know that today I struggled to get out of bed, every minute asking myself how many hours before I get to lay back down? Did you hear me use that sort of language when I stood at the stove making your dinner?"

Jackson hung his head. "No, Ma."

"Do you think there aren't moments when I want to cuss, to raise my hand to God and say the 'F' word to him for letting me suffer with this?"

Jackson looked up to see the tears in her eyes, the anguish in her raised fist. He jumped up and embraced her, setting off a flood of tears between them both. Between sobs he told her how sorry he was, that none of it was fair and she had every right to be angry with God.

She pushed him away. "I'm not angry with God," she announced. "I'm grateful for everything He's given me." Taking a deep breath, she looked at her boys. "Enough pity party. Sit up and finish the dinner I worked so hard at." Then she turned to Jackson. "This Sunday I want you to take Boyd to church. It isn't enough for him to sit and watch services on TV with me. He needs to feel the Holy Spirit's energy direct from the pulpit. And I have to say, it might do you a bit of good, too."

"Yes, Ma," he said quietly. He was glad to oblige.

* * *

As Jackson stepped into Boyd's room on Sunday morning, he had to be careful not to trip over the mounds of trash on the floor. Disorder was to be expected in any young man's room, but among the usual things one might find lay broken metal objects and piles of empty boxes. It seemed as if Boyd had become a full-blown hoarder while Jackson was away.

"Wake up, Buddy," Jackson said quietly, sitting down on the bed. No response.

"C'mon, Boyd. Ma wants me to take you to church today and that means we gotta hustle. Otherwise there won't be time for breakfast. I already took care of the horses."

The body under the covers began to stir.

"I don't want to go to church," came a muffled voice.

Jackson sighed. Knowing he'd meet resistance, he had formulated a plan.

"Well, you can sleep a little longer and go straight to church, or if you get up now I'll take you to IHOP. You decide."

Suddenly Boyd shot up. "I can have banana pancakes?"

Jackson smiled. "Sure, whatever you want."

"Or blueberry?"

"Yeah, blueberry works too."

"But what if they don't have walnuts? Last time they didn't have walnuts."

Jackson certainly remembered that morning. Boyd ended up screaming profanities from under the table. Taking him out to a restaurant had always been something of a crap shoot, even when his parents were there to referee.

"I'm pretty sure IHOP will have walnuts, Buddy. But if you don't hurry and get dressed, we won't have time for breakfast. So get a move on. The bathroom's all yours."

After that he went out to his truck, listening to the radio while he waited. It was better not to hover over Boyd when you wanted him to do something. Barely into the second song Boyd was in his seat, raising serious doubts about whether his hair or teeth had been brushed. Jackson scrutinized the clothes he'd chosen. They were decent enough to pass for church wear and that was good enough for him.

Once they were on their way, Boyd asked if Lindsey was going to be at church.

Jackson had hoped Boyd wouldn't ask about Lindsey. He'd hoped they could have a nice morning without any problems.

"Sorry, Boyd, but Lindsey is still in Little Rock with her mother. They're visiting family after her doctor's appointment."

Having Down's syndrome, Lindsey was prone to heart problems and had already been through multiple surgeries. Every six months Joy took her to Children's Hospital for check-ups. It shouldn't have been any big surprise to Boyd, but Jackson noticed his demeanor change the moment he relayed the message.

"But she should be back by Wednesday," he added.

"I'm thirsty," Boyd said quietly.

Jackson looked over at him.

"We're on our way to IHOP, Buddy. You can have whatever you want to drink once we get there."

Boyd had his face turned toward the window. He repeated, "But I'm thirsty."

Here we go, Jackson thought to himself. He thought it best to ignore the comment and see if Boyd would just drop it.

"I'm thirsty," Boyd pressed.

"I heard you, Boyd. I get it. But you're just going to have to wait 'til we get to town."

"But I'm thirsty."

Jackson bristled. "Well, I'm sorry, but there's nothing I can do about it right now. Think about something else."

Punching the dashboard, albeit not very hard, Boyd demanded, "I'm thirsty, Jackson. I need a drink!"

"Now quit, Boyd, or we won't be going to IHOP at all!" Jackson tried for one last grasp at control, but it was too late. Boyd was in another zone and there was no talking him down. He repeated himself again and again while Jackson drove on. There was no way to appease him. Maybe the little general store they'd pass on the way was open, but he doubted it. As they drove by the "Closed" sign, Boyd just got louder and more agitated; begging for a drink as if he'd trudged across a desert and would surely die.

"Pleeeease," he implored. "I need a drink."

It seemed to take forever to get to the nearest grocery store. Jackson left Boyd in the truck while he ran in to grab something, anything for his brother to drink. Of course, the line in the store slowed to a snail's pace. His stomach tightened, knowing full well he might step back outside and find Boyd in any number of compromising situations. Maybe leaving him alone in the truck was not such a good idea, but what other option did he have? Trying to drag him through the store while he was throwing a fit would have been worse.

As Jackson approached the truck, he could see Boyd talking to someone through the passenger side window. It was Miss Libby, an older woman who lived down river from them. She was busy trying to reason with Boyd, an impossible feat given Boyd's unreasonableness in these situations. She didn't understand what she was dealing with and never would.

Jackson walked around, greeted Miss Libby and held up two bottles.

"'Morning, Miss Libby. Nice to see you. I got regular water and a Vitamin Water, Boyd. Pick which one you want."

"Not water!" Boyd whined through the closed window. "Orange juice!"

"Now you know you can't have orange juice, Buddy. It bothers your stomach."

That set Boyd off on yet another tantrum of kicking the dashboard and hitting the window.

Sometimes giving choices helped, and sometimes it didn't. No matter what Jackson said, or for that matter, what kind of liquids he offered, the reaction would have been the same. The tantrum had nothing to do with a drink and everything to do with Boyd's disappointment over his girlfriend going to Little Rock. As a logical person it was nearly impossible not to try a logical approach to calm him down, but Jackson found out long ago all that did was fuel his own frustration. With Boyd, once he was triggered, it was what it was, and he just had to ride it out. Logic had nothing to do with it.

"I don't know how your mother does it, Jackson," sympathized Miss Libby. "I'd be hard-pressed not to take him out to the shed myself."

Jackson caught the laugh as a cough to hide any disrespect. Miss Libby stood no more than 4'9" in her best Sunday heels. Boyd on the other hand, with his large ears, frizzy hair and long freckled face resembled some sort of oversized leprechaun, standing just over six feet. The thought of Miss Libby trying to drag him out to the wood shed for a proper whooping was an amusing picture. She would have needed a fork lift to get him anywhere he didn't want to go.

"Well, thanks for trying to calm him down, Miss Libby. I appreciate you keeping an eye on him while I was in the store."

He was hoping a word of thanks would be enough to send her on her way. Boyd was now taunting him through the window with the keys he had so foolishly left behind.

"Well, I'll tell you what," the woman went on, "we at the Devotional Bible Church have been quite concerned about your family. You know, we are your neighbors, and being Christians, well, of course we want what's best for y'all. There isn't a soul in our congregation who didn't have compassion for your daddy. We all had sympathy for his circumstance even though his final act was a sinful one. But not a one of us can imagine why in Heaven's name your momma continues to care for that boy. I reckon that's why you're back again, and you're doing the right thing for your momma, I attest. But how are you supposed to go about the business of making a good Christian life? How are you supposed to find a proper wife for yourself when most sound women would turn and run the minute they witnessed his carryin' on? It's just not right! It's not even Christian. The Lord meant to punish that girl for her wickedness by giving her a wretch, and now here you are, bearing her burden! We commend you, Jackson for being such a good boy and coming to your momma's rescue and all, but not a one of us would blame you if you found him a suitable home in some facility or somethin' like that."

Jackson was caught somewhere between a laugh and a scream. While the woman went on with her Bible-thumping ignorance, igniting anger in the pit of his stomach, over her shoulder Boyd sat taunting him with the keys while singing, "Look wha-at I got." The juxtaposition of the two made an absurd moment even more bizarre.

Attempting composure, he put on a smile. Not a friendly one, but a forced, patient smile, the kind you save for people you aren't allowed to insult, but want to anyway.

"I appreciate your concern, Miss Libby," Jackson began, "but Boyd and Ma and I are just fine. In fact, we're better than fine. So you can tell your congregation at the Devotional Bible Church not to worry about us. We really don't need y'all's concern. In fact, we'd prefer it if y'all didn't concern yourselves with us at all."

With that, the woman stiffened, caught off guard by the rejection of her sound advice, along with Boyd changing his taunting over to, "No church! No church!"

"Well now, I know your mother and daddy never taught you to be rude!" She shot back at him. "And like it or not, as Christians, we'll be saying extra prayers for both y'all's souls!"

All Jackson could do was shrug his shoulders in response. He certainly didn't want to be pulled into a war with the members of the Devotional Bible Church. He'd passed the abandoned gas station with the garish lighted cross enough times on his travels through the back country to give him a sense of their religious beliefs. He imagined they might retaliate by letting loose on him all those snakes they danced with on Saturday nights. It was strange to think they even prayed to the same God.

As Miss Libby huffed away, mumbling to herself about rudeness and sin, Jackson walked back to the driver's side of the truck. Boyd was yucking it up while jingling the keys at him.

"All right, Boyd, you're hilarious, but enough is enough. I think church service is off the table today, but if you still want to go to IHOP, you've got to open the door."

The lock popped. With a chuckle, he shook his head.

It was disappointing not being able to take Boyd to church. Not because he'd been unable to control the situation, he'd learned a long time ago that control was a fluid thing with Boyd. The disappointment he felt came from a quiet place inside him, a part of him which was looking forward to the comfort he expected to feel once he stepped inside the sanctuary of the church. The last time he'd been inside was the day of his father's funeral.

In the time he'd been away Jackson had allowed himself to forget about God, had, in fact, left Him behind along with everyone else. As easy as it was to appreciate the wonder of His accomplishments in the beauty of softly carved sandstone or tapered columns of calcium salts, there had been no dialogue between the two, no gratitude for a job well done, no whisper of promise. It was yet another relationship ended with his father's death. Until now, he hadn't realized how much he'd missed it.

THE MOTHER OF ALL TRIGGERS

7

Thank goodness IHOP had walnuts. After breakfast, the brothers returned home with plans of an afternoon fishing at the river. When they'd left that morning Ma was in bed. The stillness which greeted them when they returned meant she was still there.

Jackson knocked softly on her door before entering the darkened room.

"Ma? You still sleeping? We brought you some pancakes and sausage."

He heard a rustle before the light came on, reassuring him she was not dead. He didn't know why he would think she was dead. Nobody had said anything about that possibility. People with MS lived long lives. Just not comfortable ones.

Boyd shuffled past him and jumped up on the far side of her bed.

"Morning, Ma." He propped himself up on the pillow next to her and began explaining why he and Jackson never made it to church. Of course he blamed the whole thing on Miss Libby, who was "bothering" them in the parking lot. "She kept on talking about me and Daddy, and finally Jackson got mad and gave her what for."

"Is that right?" Ma sniffed. "I'm guessing she deserved "what for", or your brother never would have been so rude to one of our neighbors."

Jackson felt the stare bore right through him. He nodded, and Ma's unspoken grasp of the situation became clear.

"Some people just don't know their place," she said, adjusting herself. She accepted the Styrofoam container of pancakes and sausage. Then she turned to Boyd. "But that's the last time you keep your brother from doing something I ask him to do. He was supposed to take you to church and now he's going to have to make it up to me and so are you. I'm thinking you two are going to make me a fine supper today, but first you'll have to go and catch it. A pretty rainbow trout Jackson can put on the grill. It's time we opened the grill up for the season anyway, don't you think?"

Boyd beamed with joy, having no idea how smart his mother actually was.

Jackson knew, though, and gave her a kiss on the forehead for it. Then he turned on the TV and let them watch what was left of Sunday services together.

*　*　*

Later, they settled in to Boyd's favorite spot about 100 yards from the bridge, where the river created a pool perfect for fly fishing. Jackson watched his brother's steady back and forth motion and then tried casting himself. It was obvious how out of practice he was and Boyd almost fell over laughing every time Jackson got his line caught up in a bush or a low branch. Clearly he needed to work on his technique. Fly fishing was supposed to be relaxing. Whatever this was, was not.

After a while he gave up fighting the line and just let it float out in the water, taking in his surroundings. Spring was making headway, with bright green buds lining themselves up along the wild raspberry canes. In a few weeks, their leaves would hide the thorns which would catch their clothes and tear their skin as they walked the path to the river. Kentucky warblers and American Goldfinches flitted between serviceberry and birch, bluff and beach. And then there were the Grackles, plentiful and noisy, who staked out entire rows of pines like a wild family party taking over a picnic area.

As Jackson followed the sounds back upstream, his eye parked at the center of the bridge, riveted on the metal rail his father stepped up on to before throwing himself forward into the cold, dark rush of water. The image of him doing just that played out in his head. He heard the splash, then watched his father's lifeless body float past him on the current.

Or was the image in his head wrong? Had his father actually struggled to stay afloat, drowning in the tangle of debris he was later found in? Jackson had never allowed himself to think past the jump, but what if he'd still been alive as the current pulled him along? Had he changed his mind after hitting the water and tried to swim for safety? Or had he been so determined to end it all he allowed himself to sink below the surface and drown? He resisted the urge to play each scenario out in his head, but the impulse was strong.

"Does it ever bother you, Boyd? Seeing that damn bridge every day, I mean," he said to his brother.

Boyd shrugged.

Jackson shook his head. "I don't know how I'm going to... I mean, I can't get past it, Boyd. How do you cross it every day and not think about it?" Unable to look away from the very spot where his father took his life, he went on with his question. "You wake up in the morning, every morning, and you come out of the house and there it is," he said, pointing at the bridge. "The constant reminder. The mother of all triggers. How do you do it, Boyd? How does Ma do it?"

Boyd looked at him and then up to the bridge, scrunching up one side of his face. Then he looked back at Jackson. "That's how we get to the mill," he explained.

Jackson sighed in frustration. He wasn't sure Boyd understood what he was talking about. Maybe he didn't think deeply enough or feel the sorrow deeply enough to know what he meant.

"I don't think you understand what I'm saying, Boyd. Maybe it's different for you, but I can't get it out of my head."

"I know what you're meaning," he said rolling his eyes. "I just don't mind thinkin' about him. Ma don't mind neither. We think about him ever day. We pray to Jesus ever time we walk across. I ask Jesus to give his soul a good place to rest. Not sure about Ma."

Jackson was impressed with his brother's ability to get past his grief. It seemed both Boyd and Ma had come so much further than he'd been able to in all this time.

"What do you remember about that night?" Jackson asked.

"Wasn't just that night. It was the whole week. I 'member all the fighting. And then he cussed at Ma in the mill and he cussed at me when I ran away. Then he was cussing at you on the bridge."

"You heard us?"

Boyd shook his head. "Couldn't hear the words, but I saw you. I was right here." He pointed to the ground.

"You were down here in the dark? Are you crazy? You know there are water moccasins, Boyd! It's not safe in the dark. We've talked about that a million times."

Boyd shrugged his shoulders. "He was scarier than any cottonmouth I ever seen, yelling at everbody like that. And he was... mean drunk." He whispered it as if he were embarrassed to admit it.

Jackson put down his rod and stepped over to his brother. "I'm sorry you were scared, Boyd. I was scared too. You didn't hear anything we said?"

Boyd shook his head, shoving his thumbnails between his teeth, his weight beginning to shift from one foot to the other. "Uh-unh. But I could see you. The moon was shiny. Your head was down most of the time. When you walked away that's when he jumped."

Jackson replayed the sound of the railing recovering from his father's weight. "Did you see him hit the water?"

Boyd pulled his hands away from his mouth, continuing to shift back and forth. "It was too dark. But I heard him go past." He pointed to the river. "His arms were flapping and he went by so fast. I didn't know what to do, Jackson. I was too scared. I shoulda jumped in, but it was too fast." The weight shifting had turned into a full on rocking motion, Boyd's fists jamming up against his mouth. "I'm sorry."

Jackson wanted to hug Boyd, to comfort him and calm him, but the best he could do was put his hand on his brother's shoulder. Boyd was the last person who should bear any guilt. "There's nothing you could have done to save him, Boyd. If you'd jumped in after him, you would have drowned too, and then where would we be? Huh? And he didn't yell at you because you did anything wrong that night. He was in a lot of pain and he took it out on you, and Ma, and me, too. I think he was trying on purpose to make us all mad at him. Maybe he thought it would make it easier for us somehow. He knew what he was going to do, I think he even waited for all the rain so the river would be high. I should have realized what he was doing, but I didn't want to think it was true. He was so damn determined. But it wasn't your responsibility, Boyd. He made a very bad decision and I was the one who should have stopped him."

Instead I did just the opposite, he thought.

Jackson patted Boyd's arm to calm him. He never should have brought it up. Maybe saying a prayer each time he walked across the bridge gave Boyd enough comfort to be able to do it, to keep his mind from reliving the whole incident, allowing him to go on. But maybe Boyd wasn't as "over it" as Jackson thought. There was no timetable for grief. Three years later and Jackson was barely dealing with it himself.

"I'm sorry I brought it up. We should just go back to fishing." Changing the subject, he asked, "How many fish you got in that bucket so far?"

With a toothy grin, Boyd proudly lifted up two rainbow trout. His favorite subject. Once another was caught, they packed up and headed back to the house to start the grill.

At least they accomplished one thing Ma asked of them that day.

A VISIT WITH NANA
AND PAPAW

8

Now that the grass was beginning to grow again, the fields were in dire need of mowing. Riding the mower was one of the more relaxing chores of living in the country as far as Jackson was concerned. Even with the sound of the engine roaring, it was a peaceful, mindless job he had always looked forward to.

The more bothersome job of weed eating around the flowerbeds and trees near the house could be saved for later. His plan was to mow the field across from the house and around the family cemetery before dinner.

As he opened the double doors of the tool shed he was forced to take a step back. Clearly Boyd's hoarding wasn't confined to his room. In fact, it seemed to Jackson that his hoarding was becoming something serious. The mower was barely visible beneath the debris piled high around it. Empty boxes and bicycle parts, an old station wagon fender and the blades of a rusty fan rested on top of it. Stacked high and precarious were hundreds of newspapers and Ma's discarded craft magazines. No way had she put them there.

She'd always saved the pages she wanted in a binder and recycled the rest. Boyd must have plucked them from the recycle bin.

There should have been a row of yard tools like shovels and rakes along the north wall of the shed, but there was no evidence of any of them now. In their places, hung on their hooks were links of chain and rusty pieces of... Jackson wasn't even sure what.

"Damn, Boyd," he said as he pulled trash from atop the mower. "The seat better not be ruined."

Jackson sighed with relief when he uncovered the intact seat his butt would be parked on for the next few hours. Other than the carcasses of long dead fiddlebacks under the protective tarp, he found nothing to indicate anything other than disuse. Good thing, or Boyd would get an earful. Well, more of an earful than he was already going to get for this mess. And the one in his room.

Jackson checked the tank for gas, jumped aboard and turned the engine over after a few sputtering starts. Then he backed it out, added some fresh gasoline to the tank and was on his way.

After a few passes out in the sun he was forced to remove his flannel shirt and was nearly tempted to go shirtless except for the dirt and grass seed he knew would end up sticking to his damp skin. During all his time caving, dust and chiggers were the last things he worried about coming in contact with. Living in such a pristine environment had certainly changed his standard of personal cleanliness. The t-shirt would stay on.

As he mowed his way around the cemetery, he stopped to say hello to Nana and Papaw. Finding peace in the quiet of the resting place of those who came before him was something he'd done throughout his life.

He entered the walled area and headed right to Papaw's grave, which was next to Nana's. Crouching down, he ran his hand along the smooth surface of the grey marble, following the chiseled name of *Paul Edward Hawking, Loving Husband of Charlene, Father of Paul Jr.*

and Trevor. Then he sat in between the headstones of Paul and Charlene, resting his back against the side of Papaw's stone.

"I sure do miss your chocolate biscuits and gravy, Nan. I'll have to ask Ma for the recipe so I can make them for her and Boyd. They were his favorite too. Y'all haven't heard from me for a while, you probably know I've been away. Got back a few days ago. I'm sorry to say things have gotten pretty bad around here. I'm hoping I'll be able to make it better, but I don't know.

"You probably weren't too happy with my leaving in the first place, Papaw, but I felt like I had to take care of some things for Dad. Do some of the things he always dreamed about, you know? I think he deserved as much. You never understood why he wasn't happy here, but he had every right to want more from his life. It was wrong for everyone to make him feel so trapped here. All it did was make him hate the place more and resent y'all for it." He sighed.

"There's so much out there in the world, Pap. You'd be amazed. Beautiful places that take your breath away. That was all he wanted. The chance to see it for himself. I'm not trying to make you feel bad about anything, Pap. You had your reasons for feeling the way you did. He had his. I just want you to know he wasn't wrong. That's all."

He sat for a while and listened to the breeze, wishing he had stuck up for his father back when he would hear Papaw arguing with him. Unfortunately, Jackson's mindset had always been closer to his grandfather's and once his father started drinking, he had a hard time defending anything the man said.

As he got up to go, he glanced over at the headstone marked *Trevor John Hawking.* There was no desire to go to it or trace the letters with his hand, only a desire to avoid the remorse he felt in seeing it at all. It made him want to leave, and quickly, with a promise to return to clear out the wild raspberries beginning to take over that corner of the cemetery.

ONE MAN'S TREASURES

9

Jackson shook his head as he pushed the shed doors closed. He barely fit the mower in and had things fall over on him while doing it. He was pissed and Boyd was going to hear about this for sure.

As soon as he got back to the house, he sought Boyd out. The water running in the sink, along with happy humming in the bathroom reminded him it was Wednesday. Boyd was getting ready for his girl Lindsey to arrive.

Wednesday nights were church nights, with pot luck dinners and lots of activities. Ma and Joy, Lindsey's mom, had arranged a sort of standing date for the two lovebirds every Wednesday for a few hours before church. It gave them a chance to spend time together and then be able to end that time in a more structured environment. This was good for Boyd because he had the tendency to find ways to get himself in trouble otherwise. Giving him a specific time frame kept him from going off the deep end when it was time to part company.

Jackson took the opportunity to head straight to Boyd's bedroom and begin throwing some of that trash out. He was determined to break his brother of this obsession before it became a health hazard.

"Hey!" came Boyd's voice from the door. "That's my stuff!"

Jackson lifted up a discarded soda carton. "Junk, Boyd. This is trash. All these boxes and pieces of rusty metal, they're trash. I can't believe Ma lets you do this. We'll have bugs if you keep this up. Is that what you want? Cockroaches crawling all over you when you sleep?"

Boyd's fists pressed against his mouth as he began to rock back and forth.

"It's mine. I'm going to-"

"To what? Make something out of it? Save it for the apocalypse? What? It all needs to go, along with all the crap you've got stashed out in the shed. I about broke my neck trying to get to the lawnmower just now. And where are all the tools? Buried underneath all that junk?"

"It's not junk!" Boyd yelled and lunged at Jackson, pushing him back into the pile of trash.

Jackson got up, ready for a fight. It wouldn't have been the first time he and his brother tussled over a difference of opinion. In fact, he regretted teaching Boyd how to wrestle after a particularly destructive tantrum where Jackson's only recourse was to take his brother down to avoid anyone being injured. The only one with black and blues to show for the skirmish which followed was Jackson.

But Boyd wasn't in his wrestling stance, in fact, he was busy picking up his treasured junk, trying to keep Jackson from getting it.

"It's mine," he said over and over. "Not yours!"

"This is not healthy, Boyd. Not for you, or anyone else in this house. It's obviously gone on too long."

"NOT YOURS!" Boyd screamed. "NOT YOURS!" Then he began to cry, loud and melodramatic, rocking back and forth while holding as much of his treasure as he could.

"What's going on here?" Ma asked from the doorway.

"Have you seen this mess in here? He's out of control, Ma! Even the shed is trashed!"

She hobbled over to Boyd, and touched his arm. "It's okay, Boyd. Jackson was just trying to help. He doesn't understand that these are your treasures. You can put them back." She turned to Jackson. "Now leave him be."

Jackson shook his head. "No, I'm not going to let him turn this place into one of those country trash heaps. It's not how we've ever done things around here. We're not those people!" He pointed outward, toward some imaginary shack, surrounded by rusted car skeletons and years of garbage filling up the holler.

Ma's voice was restrained as Boyd continued to rock back and forth. "*You're* not going to let him? Who put you in charge? You think just because you've been back a few days that you can dictate what goes on around here? You think you have some sort of monopoly on dealing with grief and that gives you a say in other people's lives? We're all dealing with something here, Jackson, and we're all managing things in our own way. He's in mourning for his father. You ran away to find comfort. Boyd finds his in saving things most people throw away. If it makes him feel safe to have this junk all around him when he sleeps, then so be it." She picked up a headless Power Ranger and handed it to Boyd. "The shed you can clean up, even have him help you, after all, he made the mess. Then you can make it off limits to him because you need all those tools in good shape to care for the property. You have no argument from me there. But Boyd's room is his own and you're just going to have to let him be."

As much as he wanted to stand his ground, there seemed no reason to continue the argument. Ma had chosen a side.

"You hear me, Boyd?" she asked. "You'll help your brother organize that shed and then you keep out of it, understand?"

Boyd continued to hold tight to his trash, but he nodded in agreement.

"See? Good. Now go shower," she said to Jackson. "You stink and the girls are on their way." She looked her boys over and nodded, as if confirming her success in settling the argument. Then she carefully left the room.

"She's coming, Jackson!" Boyd did an off-kilter leap in the air, landed on his own foot, and knocked himself off balance. He waved his arms to right himself as his treasures fell to the floor, becoming part of the pile once more. "But no church tonight. They're too tired."

The quickness with which the situation turned was stunning. Jackson felt defeated. "No church? You must be disappointed." The only enthusiasm he could muster was in sarcasm. Ma's rebuke stung like a sweat bee.

"I'm 'a take her fishing."

"I bet that will be a surprise."

"Nah," said Boyd. "We always go fishing. 'Cept one time I took her to the cemetery to show her the stones."

"Nice," Jackson nodded. "Very romantic. When girls are scared sometimes they let you hold their hands."

Boyd giggled. "Yeah, sometimes."

"You better get yourself ready then." He shook his head and passed Boyd in an awkward embrace to keep himself from tripping along the small pathway cleared to the door.

Sometimes there were words in your mouth and you just weren't allowed to say them, which was irritating as hell.

YOU'LL BE THE FIRST ONE DOWN

10

Jackson came out to the porch, feeling a bit less aggravated after his shower. Ma was standing next to a bright blue SUV with Lindsey's mom. He could have sworn he heard his and Natalie's names being mentioned before the two women noticed him and stopped talking.

Joy smiled as he made his way down the steps.

"Your mother wasn't lying. It's the handsome Prodigal Son returned from the great wide world. Hey, Jackson. Nice to see you." She held her arms open for a hug.

Jackson returned the embrace. "Hey, Joy. Good to see you too." He looked over and saw Lindsey sitting in the passenger seat. "Hey, Sassafrass."

Lindsey crossed her arms and "Hrrumphed", turning her face away with all the dramatic flair she could muster.

"She's still mad at you for leaving," warned Joy. "Better watch out."

He stepped up to the window, begging her to open it.

"C'mon, Sassy, please? I'll be your best friend."

"You mean!" she accused him.

"Me? Mean? I'm not mean. See, I'm out here waiting for my hug. Now, do mean people wait for hugs?"

"Mean!" she said and stuck out her tongue.

"Ah, Lindsey, why are you so mad at me? I said good-bye before I left, remember?"

"Girlfriend sad," she said and Jackson knew exactly what she meant.

"Natalie? Natalie was sad after I left?"

"You mean."

"Aww, I'm sorry, Lindsey. I guess everyone was sad. I was sad then too, remember? But I'm here now. Doesn't that count for something?"

"Boyfriend?" she asked, brightening.

"Well, not exactly, but friends. Is that okay? Can me and Natalie just be friends?"

Lindsey thought about it. Then she shrugged. "Okay," she said and opened the door.

Jackson smiled when Lindsey got out of the car and wrapped her arms around him. He took advantage of the moment and pulled her up off the ground, sending her into squeals of both laughter and admonition.

"Stop!" she shrieked while playfully hitting him.

"It's so good to see you, Sassy," he said as he put her down. "I sure did miss you."

After straightening her clothes and flipping back her long brown hair, she asked, "Where Boyd?"

Jackson looked at Ma. "I thought he was out here waiting. Where'd he go?"

Ma shrugged. "That's what I thought, too."

"Well," Jackson nudged Lindsey. "He must have skipped out with the first chick who came along."

"Uh-uh." She was quick, placing her hands on her hips to emphasize the fact that she could not be fooled by his teasing.

"Uh-huh," Jackson mimicked her, hands on hips and all.

"Uh-uh," she returned.

"Okay, you two," said Joy. "This could go on for hours."

"Just kidding," Jackson admitted. "He was chompin' at the bit. Maybe he's still in the house making himself handsome for you."

"Eww." Lindsey contorted her face in mock disgust.

"Yeah, I'm with ya on that," he agreed, "but somehow we love him anyway, don't we?"

It had been so long since he'd felt like playing with anyone. Who knew acting like a six year old could feel so good?

"Lindsey!" Boyd yelled from the side of the house. "You made it!"

He made a beeline toward Lindsey, who put up a hand to stop him.

"Too much," she told him with a shake of her head and her hand. "Chill out."

Like a well-trained puppy, he did as he was told. He took a deep breath and relaxed his body.

"Where you go?" she asked him. "New girl?"

Boyd looked around, confused by the question.

"Yeah," Jackson continued the teasing. "Where'd you go? You left your girl waiting."

Boyd shifted on his feet, seeming very uncomfortable. "Nowhere. Just. Around the house," he lied.

Jackson could tell. Boyd rarely lied, even to cover up his own mistakes. If anything, he was abnormally honest, admitting guilt when most people would be keeping their mouths shut to avoid punishment. Jackson was curious about Boyd's disappearance, but he knew better than to press the issue in front of Lindsey.

Lindsey, on the other hand, believed his lies and took his hand. "Okay," she said and they walked off together as Boyd explained how he hated when she went to the doctor because it was too far away. He even volunteered to go along for the ride next time to keep her company.

"Why don't you join us for some sweet tea?" Ma said to Joy. "You girls are welcome to stay for dinner. I'm making a big pot of chicken and noodles."

"Sounds wonderful, Ruth. I wouldn't want to break my streak of letting other people cook for me on Wednesdays."

"Jackson, why don't you keep Joy company on the porch while I get the tea? I'm sure she'd love to hear all about your travels."

After helping Ma up the steps, Jackson walked to the end of the porch and looked back toward the shed. He was sure he had pulled the doors tightly together, but now there was a gap between them. Boyd must have panicked after their conversation with Ma and run out to the shed to rescue some treasure before anyone else had a chance to throw it out.

"It's so nice to have you back," Joy reached out to pat his arm as he sat. "Are you back for good?"

He was thrown off by the loaded question and so by the time he thought of a possible answer, the awkward silence said it all. He cleared his throat instead.

"Sooo," she said uncomfortably, "then maybe you can just tell me where your travels took you?"

You mean before I became frozen with fear and gave up all hope? He thought, and then decided to settle himself into a more social posture. Joy was a guest come to visit and she had every right to expect niceties and sweet tea, not be drawn into the family drama.

"I got to see a lot of places, actually. South America, Bermuda, we even explored a cave in Barbados." This was the first time since he'd been home that anyone pressed him to talk about his caving experiences. He'd been so distracted with everything else he'd almost forgotten about them himself. "But not all the great caves are far away. The United States has quite a few places to explore too – like Carlsbad Caverns or Kartchner out in Arizona. I've got pictures if you want to see." He pulled his phone from his pocket.

"Awesome!" Joy inched closer. "I'd love to see them."

Jackson held the phone out between them and began scrolling through various pictures, recalling their locations and sometimes how he got the shot.

Joy stopped him at one in particular. "What is that?"

Jackson had tried to scroll past it, and swallowed hard when she swiped back to it.

I should have deleted it. "It's the last cave I explored."

"You were that high up?"

The shot looked down into a lushly vegetated sink hole with thick vines clinging to the walls.

"Yeah, it's almost four hundred feet down." Sweat beads formed along his hair line. "It was pretty crazy."

"You climbed down those walls?"

A bead of sweat tickled at his temple. He wiped it away. "We actually had to repel into the pit. I'm hanging upside down in this picture. My teammate Rob was holding my harness so he could pull me back up once I got the shot."

"That's frightening," said Joy.

Jackson agreed. "In caving, you can never let your guard down. You always have to be paying attention and taking mental pictures of what lies ahead. You have to put each foot forward, but not put your weight down until you knew for sure it's solid ground under that foot. It's incredibly easy to forget yourself in the darkness, and very deadly." He looked at the picture and swallowed hard.

A burning in his stomach radiated upward toward his chest. He swallowed again to tamp it down. The moment captured by this picture had stunned him as only one other moment in his life had. It had halted his mission. In that instant he learned just how lethal he might be to himself, and vowed to keep his feet solidly above ground ever after. He would never enter another cave as long as he lived. Pushing away the compulsion to dwell on it, he swiped the picture away.

"You all right?" asked Joy.

He choked and nodded, then coughed away the answer. "Fine, something stuck in my throat."

Suddenly Ma's voice broke in. "Would you mind grabbing the glasses off the counter for me?" She hobbled over with the pitcher of tea, using a chair for balance instead of her cane.

Jackson got up. "No, of course not," and stepped inside.

When he got back out to the porch, Ma and Joy were busy looking through his photos. He poured them each a glass of tea.

Joy swiped through another round of pictures.

"You always had a partner?"

"Definitely," Jackson answered, wishing to move on. "At first I studied with this guy. Wait, let me find a good picture. There, that guy," he pointed to a bearded man in full climbing gear. "And then once he thought I knew my stuff, he helped me find a team to travel with. These guys were my team," he said, showing her a different picture.

"Why haven't you shown me any of these pictures since you've been back?" asked Ma.

He shrugged. "The subject hasn't really come up," he answered. *It's not really my favorite subject*, he thought.

Unwilling to admit that to his mother, who would then be full of questions, he mustered some enthusiasm for her. "This one was taken in Stephen's Gap, right there in Alabama. Just a day's drive away." Then he showed her how to scroll through the other pictures, stopping at the ones he thought she'd be interested in. "This was our group in Carlsbad. You see how big this room is? It's incredible, really. Millions of bats live there. Boyd would love it."

"I'm sure he would," replied Ma.

"Which cave was your favorite?" asked Joy.

None anymore, he thought. He took a breath and resolved to get through this conversation without pulverizing into a puddle of weak gelatinous puke. *Remember when you weren't a coward?*

"Well, the sinkholes are breathtaking because of the vegetation hanging over the sides and the depth on some of them is insane. Repelling down into them is, I don't know, like you're suspended in time. You can feel the cool air around you, and you're so aware of the walls and the rock. When you get to the bottom it's like being in another world. You half expect some dinosaur to come out of the vines and start chasing you." Taking a sip from his glass, he immersed himself in a happy memory. "Dad always loved the caves where we had to squeeze ourselves through small cracks in the wall, but Boyd and I were never sure if we were going to make it through, you know, it's so easy to get yourself caught on stuff and nobody wants to be the guy to panic. Of course, if we'd really thought about it, we would have realized Dad was way bigger than we were, and if he made it through a tight spot, we were golden, but being young and stupid, we'd always have that freak out moment. Those tight places were always a challenge for me. Maybe that's why I liked the big rooms, in the caves like Mammoth that open up wide and tall. I was always relieved when I got to them."

When he looked back to Ma, he realized she had tears in her eyes.

"What's wrong, Ma?"

She lovingly held the phone to her chest.

"You know he took me with him a few times to some of the local caves."

He shook his head. "You never said anything about it."

"I hated it," she said with complete candor. "My claustrophobia set in and all I could think about was the ceiling caving in on me. One time I had a full-fledged panic attack and I made him take me home. I could tell he was disappointed."

"So you never went after that?"

"Nope. He never invited me, which, when you think about it, was probably dangerous because then he'd go alone. I felt bad, not offering to go along, but I was too scared I'd freak out again. As soon as you boys were old enough he started taking you with him and that made me feel better."

"Those were the best days," Jackson recalled with a sigh. "I don't understand why he stopped. Even when we were a pain in the butt he still seemed to be having a good time."

Ma was quiet, but Jackson could tell she wanted to say something. He waited.

"Don't you ever say this to your brother," she waved a finger at him, "but it was because of Boyd. He was getting harder to handle and your father was afraid he would get hurt. He considered just taking you, but imagine how devastated Boyd would have been seeing you two go off without him. It wore on him for a long time. So don't think it wasn't because he didn't enjoy going with you boys. He loved those outings."

"I don't think I ever felt as close to him as I did during those adventures," said Jackson. "And I don't think we were ever as close after that. It was the one thing we had in common. The only thing. That's why I thought –" He thought about the last few years and his failure to accomplish his one goal. "I tried so hard to get that back," he said as his eyes filled with tears.

Ma took his hand. "You know, Jackson, when you left I thought you were just trying to get away from all of us. That we were too much of a burden for you to carry with the weight of his death on your shoulders. But I realize now that it wasn't about us, it was about him. You were out there looking for him all this time, weren't you?"

Jackson nodded.

Problem is, I never did find him, Ma. He came close to saying it out loud.

AN UNWELCOME IDEA

(Not to be confused with an unwelcome thought)
11

I t was a sleepless night for Jackson, unable to choose a side to sleep on, trying to better understand why his mission had been a sham. As hard as he looked and as close as he listened, he hadn't found his father in any of the caves he'd explored. How could he tell his mother that after all the time he spent time waiting for a sign, a dream, even a whisper in his ear, that when the whisper finally came, it frightened him so much he spent the last nine months working the docks of the Mississippi, disappointed with himself and unsure how to move on, afraid to return home?

Tired of the same old fears swirling in his head, he turned his attention to his laptop, researching the intricacies of his mother's disease (of which there were many). He hoped there was something he might be able to do in order to help her.

Every case of Multiple Sclerosis he read about seemed as different as the person represented. The type of MS his mother had, Primary Progressive, was a steadily progressing, ultimately debilitating disease. It would most likely put her in a wheelchair before eventually confining her to a bed. Her wit and wisdom might stay intact, and then again, in the fickleness of the disease, it might not. Her eyesight could go without warning, as well as her ability to talk or swallow.

There were so many variables, it was overwhelming to think about. One thing was for sure. There would come a time when Ma would need constant care. Some people went to nursing homes, which was understandable when it became too hard for family members to care for them. He'd be damned if his mother was going to end up in one of those places. He would do everything in his power to make sure that didn't happen.

The glaring question then, was, who would pay for it? Was she even insured for long term care? He remembered how Papaw's illness had put a strain on the family finances during his battle with cancer. He wasn't going to make the same mistake. Jackson had to make sure his family was taken care of. The time for a conversation with his mother was now, before it was too late to make the right choices. In fact, it might already be too late. He hoped he wouldn't need to consider any drastic options.

* * *

After breakfast the next morning, he told Boyd to go on and feed the horses, and he would meet him later at the mill.

He cleared off the table and stood beside Ma at the sink while she washed the breakfast dishes.

As he pulled a towel from the drawer to dry them, she looked him up and down.

"What do you need?" She asked.

"I don't need anything," he began and then backtracked. "Well, I do need to talk to you. It's serious stuff. Do you feel up to it?"

Looking up at him, she smirked. "That bad? Have at it."

Now that he had her attention, he was at a loss as how to begin. He continued to dry dishes as she washed.

"Well?" she prompted him. "Just start somewhere."

"I've been doing some thinking."

"Oh boy, watch out!" she teased. As she finished wiping out the sink, she asked, "Seems like this might take a while. Do you mind if I sit down?"

"No, not at all." He took her arm and helped her to the table, where she would be more comfortable.

"Okay, so tell me what you've thinking about. Is this about yesterday?" She fiddled with her placemat.

"No, well, it's not about Dad, or caves or anything like that. It's about you and what's in store for you medically and how we're going to handle those things."

"We? Are you part of this now?" She stopped fiddling.

"Well, yes, of course. I'm your son. I care about you and Boyd and what happens to you both. I-I don't want to get caught up in a conversation about the past, Ma. This is about the future – your future, Boyd's future. Even my future. We need to plan for the inevitable and how we're going to deal with it."

"What do you think is so inevitable?" She asked it without any playfulness in her voice.

Jackson was stunned. She had to have considered this before. He knew what he was thinking, but he struggled to say it. Knowing where his mother was going to end up and saying it out loud to her were two entirely different things. It was as if, by speaking the words, he would be condemning her to a wheelchair or worse. And it didn't seem as if she was going to make it any easier for him by giving him the words. How did doctors look their patients in the eye and tell them things like this?

Just say it, damn it!

"You know, this disease progresses. Eventually, the cane won't be enough and you'll need a walker or a wheelchair. And someday you'll need someone to come in and take care of you. To help you take showers and care for yourself. Are you covered for things like that, Ma? Have you thought about how you would pay for it?"

She seemed unfazed. "Well, I have insurance. They pay for my doctors and most of my medicine."

He nodded. "Yeah, for now. But they won't pay for any experimental drugs the doctors might want to try, and they'll probably only pay for a certain number of therapy sessions, which you should really be going to already. God forbid you fall and end up in the hospital..."

"Jackson Bryer Hawking! What are you trying to do to me? Are you wishing these things upon me?"

"Of course not, Ma. If it was up to me, none of this would be happening to you! But we have to be realistic. And we have to come up with a plan so we don't get taken by surprise later. There's nothing wrong with thinking ahead."

This was a difficult conversation already, but he wasn't done.

"I want to talk to you about options, and I know you're going to freak out about it, but one of those options is selling the mill to help pay for the things you'll need."

She stared at him for a moment, then shook her head, insisting, "No!"

"Listen to me, Ma, selling the mill might protect it in the end."

"Let me rephrase that. Hell, no!"

He sighed, looking around the room, asking for help from someone, anyone. Of course, there was no one else.

"What do you think is going to happen when you run out of money and your medical expenses get too high? They're going to take it all away, you know that, don't you? They'll take everything you own to pay off your debt."

"No! I'm not selling any of it!"

He took her hands to calm her.

"Okay, okay, I know, this sucks. You don't need to make any decisions right now. I just want you to start thinking about it, that's all."

"I don't have to think about it. I already know my answer. And just where are you in all this? Are you on your way back out the door, or is it your intention to stay and be part of the family again?"

"I'm here right now, Ma."

What he meant, he didn't know, wasn't really ready to put words to it. The commitment to stay was a fluid, shapeless notion in his mind. He found himself unable to give it any form or substance.

Unable or unwilling? Even Jackson was unsure.

Her eyes teary, she asked, "What happened to you? You used to love this place. You were such a happy kid."

"What happened to me? April 26th happened to me, Ma."

The night which changed everything he thought about his father, this place, and especially himself.

She reversed his hold and pulled at his hands, pleading. "What could he possibly have said to make you hate our home so much?"

Jackson turned away from her.

"It wasn't just what he said to me. I-I... Let's just say his weren't the only harsh words thrown that night." He got up to leave but she held on fast.

"Jackson. You have to stop blaming yourself. You didn't make him jump. It's not your fault, Sweetheart."

"I gotta go," he said and gently pulled his hands from her.

SECOND TIME FAILS TO CHARM

12

As he approached the mill, holding back his emotion, he determined Natalie would be his best shot for an ally in this new campaign, albeit an angry one. She was a practical woman and might be resistant at first, but with a little information and some time for thought she would come around to his way of thinking.

Stepping in to the mill's gift shop, he welcomed the familiar vibration of the inner workings of the mill. The water gate had been opened. The turbines were spinning and the belts slapped and rattled overhead. Over in the corner, flour was already sliding down the chute into a blue tub.

Natalie was busy restocking shelves of milled flour. She turned to see who'd come in.

"Where's Ruth?" she asked.

"I'm sure she'll be down in a minute," Jackson said as he stepped closer. "I wanted to talk to you before she got here."

"What could there possibly be for us to talk about? You haven't humiliated me enough?"

Her sarcastic tone confused him.

"I humiliated you? Here I thought I was the one who embarrassed myself. I must be a bigger asshole than I thought."

"Self-awareness is a healthy thing," she said and went back to stocking the shelf. "A deeper analysis might do you some good."

"Hehe. Yeah, I get it. You're mad at me. You should be."

"Then you'll understand why I'd rather not be around you, right? We may work in the same building, but that doesn't mean we have to see each other. You can stay in your space and I'll stay in mine. I would appreciate that if we do run into each other you don't try to talk to me."

A deep cut even if it was deserved.

Natalie grabbed the empty box at her feet and stormed off toward the back room.

"Natalie?"

Throwing the box down, she turned and narrowed her eyes at him.

"What about 'don't talk to me' do you not get?"

Jackson held his hand out to stop any further aggression.

"I know, it's just that, well, I have a favor to ask you."

He watched Natalie's face change from pissed off to something else, more like a sneeze coming on.

Then she burst into a genuine laugh.

Jackson squirmed.

"You're funny," she said, shaking a finger at him.

He ignored her response and forged ahead. "Listen, I know how you think, well, at least I used to, and you were always very practical. And my mother trusts your judgment. If you can put aside your hatred for me and look at the big picture you might come to the same conclusion I did. Then she might listen to you." He pulled in a deep breath. "I need you to convince Ma to sell the mill."

Natalie stopped smiling. In fact, she stood very quietly, as if considering the notion Jackson had presented. Then she walked toward him with purpose and jabbed a finger into his chest.

"If you think I'm going to try to convince your mother to sell the one thing that brings her joy, you are out of your mind. This mill is all she has left. She used to ride her horses, but she can't anymore. She used to enjoy the walk from her house to this shop, but now she has to drive. She used to go into town to visit with friends, but now she avoids it like the plague. Little by little, everything has been taken from her." With eyes piercing his being, she admonished him. "Not this. You can't take this away from her. This is her life. She loves this place. She thrives on helping people and talking to customers who want to know about the history of the area. You should see her when she directs them to the sights around here. She lights up like a sparkler." She pointed to an area behind him. "You see the Crafter's Corner there? With the beautiful pottery and blown glass? That was her idea and something your father refused to let her try. Not only is it a great success, but she supports local artists and in return, she brings money into the mill. More money than he ever did."

She stepped over to shelves marked "Organic" and picked up a bag of biscuit mix.

"You see this? All these mixes and recipes were her idea, and her idea to market them as organic was genius considering everyone is looking for organic now. It's not as if she's been stationary since you've been gone. This mill is her business and it's a good one. It's where she draws her strength from. I'm not going to talk her into anything. With everything she's been through, she deserves to spend as much time as she can doing the things that make her happy."

Jackson wanted to agree with everything Natalie said, but none of it changed the reality of the situation.

"And what if everything she owns gets taken away to pay for her medical expenses? Then what, Natalie? It happens all the time, you know. People lose their houses, their land..."

She rolled her eyes. "All she has to do is put it all in your name. Then they can't take a dime from her."

A silent moment passed between them.

Jackson's face betrayed his guilt.

"Oh, I get it," she said. "You'd sell it anyway. That's how much you hate this place. I see." She took in a breath and let her attention be drawn to the drawstring of the biscuit mix, playing with the knot. "I'm so sorry he did this to you, Jackson. It makes me so mad to think about the trauma he caused you with his selfishness. Why couldn't he have just jumped from that damn bridge and left you out of it? Why did he have to go around terrorizing you all before he did it? Fuck him! Fuck him and his self-pity! The fact that he never appreciated what he had here is sickening to me. And the fact that in the time he had with you that night he managed to turn you to the dark side makes me angry as hell." She squeezed the bag and pointed it at him. "You used to love this place! I remember how proud you were to show me around and take me to all your "secret spots". You remember playing hide and seek with Boyd on rainy days? Or our walks along the river? Have you forgotten your favorite Mimosa tree? Either you were the best liar ever, or he did such a number on you-" she stopped herself and changed direction, turning back toward the shelf. "Whatever he said to you was bullshit and I wish you could see what it's done to you. Fuck him. Fuck your idea. That's all I have to say."

He wasn't surprised by Natalie's strong rebuke of his father, it wasn't the first time she'd shared her feelings on the subject. In fact, she wasn't the only one to express her opinion back then.

Some people took his father's decision to end his life very personally. There were those who pulled Jackson aside in the days following his father's death to convey their deep sorrow and regret for not doing more, and still others who talked of a need for understanding and compassion. But there were also many who were angered by Trevor's suicide. The selfishness it took and his thoughtlessness for those he left behind pissed a lot of people off. Natalie was one of those people. Jackson allowed her to voice her opinion, but just like those others, she was wrong. Even he was wrong at first.

"That's exactly what I did say," Jackson said quietly. "Before he jumped. I told him to go fuck himself. I told him to please put us all out of his misery and jump."

"Really?" She turned to face him. "You never told me that."

"I never told anyone. And you know the worst part? Even with everything he said that night, even though he told me exactly what he was going to do, I never thought he'd really do it." He shook his head as if he still couldn't believe it, his attention drawn to the image in his head. "But he did, as soon as I walked away. He said, "Watch me", and then I heard the railing give. When I turned back, he was gone." For a moment he paused, running through the memory, surprised by the raw truth shaking loose over the past few days. "What if he did it out of spite for what I said? I'll never forget the last words I said to him. I'll never forgive myself for saying them."

"Don't do that," Natalie stepped closer. "The decision was his. It wouldn't have mattered what you said, he'd already made up his mind."

Jackson shrugged and pursed his lips. "Maybe. And maybe not. Maybe he was waiting for a reason *not* to do it. What if what he really wanted was for me to come up with an argument to prove he was wrong? What if he was waiting for me to give him reasons to live?"

Natalie had no response. Even she lacked the words.

None of it mattered now. There was nothing Jackson could do except hold himself accountable for his part in his father's death.

He wiped the emotion from his face. "Anyway, it's not about hating the place, it's about doing what's right for my mother and Boyd. Sooner or later she's going to need a lot of care. If her money's going to run out, I'd rather she take the time to get a good price for the place and not get screwed later on because there's a rush to sell it all."

Outside, a car crunched the gravel alongside the building.

"That's her. I'll go help her in. Do me a favor please and research some of this stuff before you shrug it off. Look up the potential cost of medical care for MS patients like her and some of their personal stories and then decide. I'm not trying to be the bad guy here, Nat. Just a realist."

Without waiting for a response he was off to help Ma maneuver the steps leading to the shop.

He ran out to her and as he took his mother's arm he told her of an idea she might be happy with.

"I'm going to take out these stairs and build a ramp here. Then the shop will be wheelchair accessible, which should be code, anyway. What do you think?"

"Well now," she said, "making improvements. Yes, that's something I *can* agree to."

Jackson smiled. *One victory at a time.* Even if it was a small one.

MOSES AT THE CROSSROADS

13

The second attempt at church service went much smoother than the first. Boyd even managed to talk Ma into coming along since she was up early and seemed to be feeling cheery.

Jackson could feel the change in his mother's mood as they drew closer to town. She withdrew from her side of the conversation and replaced it with sighs.

"What's wrong?" he asked as he lifted her from the truck.

By the way she looked around the parking lot, he knew. She was embarrassed. She didn't want anyone to see her in this weakened state.

"Who cares what they think?" he startled her with his observation.

"What are you talking about?" she asked, grabbing her cane from the seat.

"Is this why you don't come to town? Because you don't want them to see you? Are you afraid they'll judge you? Think somehow you deserve all this?"

"It's not the judgement, son. I've had my share of those looks after your father died. You think I don't know the things they thought? 'There goes the woman whose husband would rather be dead than spend another minute with her.'"

"Ma!" Jackson was shocked by her take on what she thought people's judgments were.

"I know what goes on in people's minds. It's not that," she continued. "It's the pity. The ones who look at you with big sad eyes, and don't know what to say. I can see how uncomfortable it makes them for me to be in their presence. So, how do they think I feel?"

"But you meet people all day at the mill and it doesn't seem to bother you."

"That's different. Most of them are tourists and strangers. I'll never have to see them again. Besides, if I see pity in their eyes, I get to hold it over them because I'm dealing with an illness. They think I'm brave and I can use it to my advantage. If it helps me sell a few more bags of biscuit mix, so be it. I couldn't do that with these people, they know me too well."

"And you don't think your friends see you as brave?"

"What's so brave about walking with a cane? Does it take courage to open your eyes in the morning and get out of bed?"

Jackson thought the answer to that question was obvious. "For some people, yes, it does."

Ma pushed the thought away with her hand. "I get up because I have no other choice, not because I'm courageous. And you're right if you're thinking it took more courage for your father to go on living than it did to jump off that bridge."

"Ma! What the hell? That wasn't at all what I meant. Though I am thinking you're the one who needs some church healing today."

Again, she pushed Jackson's idea away with her hand and shook her head.

"Where's your brother?" she asked.

Jackson looked around. Boyd was nowhere to be seen.

"He must have gone in to find Lindsey."

Ma insisted on sitting toward the back of the church even though Boyd had settled himself in with Lindsey and Joy up ahead.

Jackson looked around, keenly aware of those who noticed not only him, but his mother. They either smiled and nodded a hello, or quickly turned to the person sitting next to them to pass along the gossip. In his desire to feel the comfort of being surrounded by the house of God, he'd forgotten the main reason he disliked church so much.

In his younger years it was a place to see friends, learn doctrine, and be part of something bigger. Once he was old enough to appreciate the lessons, it became a place to learn introspection – in order to determine what he needed more or less of in his daily life based on a clear moral compass. Around this same time, and to his bewilderment, he found it had become a place to judge outwardly, through gossip and condemnation of anyone who seemed guided by a compass pointed in a different direction. He did his best to steer clear of the judgmental behavior, but it was difficult. Especially if he wanted to fit in. Why did those so immersed in the Words of Jesus forget those words the second they left the building? Sometimes while they were still in it?

Caving was so different. Immersing himself in God's underground creations during the past few years had left him very little room for judgement. Cavers didn't care what you did up top, they only cared about your behavior while exploring. *Take nothing but pictures, leave nothing but footprints, kill nothing but time.* Those were the commandments he'd learned to live by. Maybe he had gotten something out of his exploration after all.

He noticed Natalie sitting up ahead on the right beside her parents. Her father eyed Jackson and nodded, then whispered something to his wife. A second later, Mrs. Shepard turned toward him and quickly looked away. He could see her nudge Natalie, no doubt to warn her of his presence, but Natalie never budged. He wondered if she had said anything to her parents about his return. After all, they might not be happy about her continuing to work at the mill if he were going to be there.

Jackson wished the service would get started already.

Singing soon filled the church and pulled him in, filling him full of memories, good and bad.

The last time he sat in this church was at his father's funeral. The pews were overflowing with friends and neighbors. He was sure his father would have been happy with the turnout.

He thought of all the times Natalie sat by his side, her hand enfolded by his. He would spend most of the time tracing her fingers with his free hand, half listening to the sermon being given.

Today the sermon was about Moses and the crossroads at which he found himself, making the decision to leave behind his station in life in order to stand with the Hebrews. Moses' decision caused great disappointment to those who loved him as their own. Pharaoh had awarded him opportunity and power by accepting him as a grandson, but he turned away from all of it, his faith unlocking the treasures of God instead.

"Great decisions are always costly," Reverend Paulsen stated.

Jackson thought of his own decision to turn his back on what was expected of him in order to feel closer to his father. Lost was the time he could have spent with his brother and mother, helping them through the mourning process. He'd lost touch with his heritage and the pride he once took in it. And he'd lost Natalie. The one person who'd allowed him to always be himself and loved him without question. This was the price he'd been willing to pay to make sense of the world crashing down around him. For all his sacrifice, had he accomplished anything of value? He certainly didn't feel any closer to knowing the truth of it. Like Moses, would he die before ever seeing the Promised Land? Would he ever find satisfaction in the decisions he'd made?

CLEANING OUT THE SHED

14

After church Ma served a brunch of chicken salad and blueberry cobbler, which the family enjoyed out on the porch. Jackson then asked Boyd to walk with him, keeping their destination a secret as they left the house. When it became obvious they were heading for the shed, Boyd's steps got slower and slower.

Jackson didn't want a repeat of the other day's standoff. "It's no big deal, Bud. We're going to go through the shed together. Anything you want to keep you can put to the side and I promise we'll find a place for it."

Boyd let out an exaggerated sigh of relief.

"But it can't be everything, you hear?" Jackson maintained. "There's more than enough trash in there to fill a dumpster."

He opened the shed and stepped back. "I'll back the mower out and then we can start on the left wall and work our way around."

Boyd was already smashing his fists against his face with anxiety. This was going to be a struggle for him.

Jackson patted his brother on the shoulder and reminded himself of Ma's instructions to be gentle about the project. She assured him it was the best way to get Boyd's cooperation.

"One thing at a time, okay?" He handed Boyd a pair of work gloves.

Boyd stopped smashing his face and looked down at the ground.

"Okay," he said as he took the gloves and put them on.

Jackson picked up the first object in his way, a plastic tub filled with hand tools.

"Here, why don't you go through these? Any ones that are broken or rusted go in that bin over there. We'll take them to the recycling place tomorrow." Maybe if he thought the tools were going on to another life he'd be okay with letting some go.

Boyd took the tub and sat in the grass, pulling out each tool and looking it over while Jackson drove the mower out of the shed. A box full of batteries spilled into the empty space.

"Are those used batteries?" Jackson asked as he made his way back.

Boyd shrugged without making eye contact.

"So, that would be a yes," he concluded and threw the box and the spilled batteries into the nearby trash bin. Then he turned back to the shed and purged what he could while Boyd was busy looking through the tools. He was surprised to find a workbench under a collection of empty paint cans and fishing gear.

"Jesus, Boyd. This is a nice bench. Bet Ma bought it for you, but I don't think this was what she had in mind for it."

Boyd looked down at the ground. Jackson had intended to inflict guilt, but now he felt bad for it. He thought about the times Papaw would do that to his father, make side remarks to ruffle Trevor's feathers. Then Trevor would get pissed off and drink out of spite, eventually taking his anger out on his family. Shit sure did roll downhill.

"How about we put up a rack for all your fishing poles?" Jackson said as a peace offering. "That way you won't get the lines all knotted up."

Boyd smiled and nodded. "I was gonna do that," he said. "Just didn't have time yet."

The sins of the father are visited on the sons for three and four generations. No wonder. Who else do we learn from but those who've gone before us?

Jackson looked at the two piles Boyd had going after 40 minutes of work. One was made up of the tools he thought they should keep. The other had one broken pair of pliers in it. "I'll take it," he said out loud. "Progress is a slow march forward."

The rest of the shed went pretty much the same way, with Jackson handing Boyd a smaller task to keep busy with while he purged what he could unnoticed.

On a table near the window Jackson found a stack of magazines addressed to Trevor Hawking. They were caving magazines filled with amazing pictures and tips on spelunking and the gear needed to do it. He imagined his father thumbing through them, dreaming of the day he might be able to have his own adventures, putting himself into the pictures, geared up and raring to go.

Boyd must have thumbed through them too, picturing their father, or Jackson for that matter, in any one of those photographs. He must have looked at them often, because there wasn't as much dust on the magazine covers as on the objects around them.

It seemed he and Boyd had been on similar paths after all, looking for a ghost who never did appear. Boyd must have been scanning the pages of the dreams his father left behind, while Jackson searched those places in real time.

Neither the photos nor the places in them managed to satisfy the need burning in Trevor Hawking's sons to know their father again, or understand his actions.

"Can you take me sometime?" Boyd's voice came from behind.

Jackson turned to see his brother looking over his shoulder. "Caving?"

Boyd nodded. "'member all those times we went with Dad? Can you take me?"

Jackson wiped the sweat from his forehead. He hadn't realized how hot it had become in the late spring afternoon.

"We could go to Sweet Spot. That was my favorite 'cause it has fish. 'member that time we brought a net and caught a pike?"

Jackson's throat began to tighten. He coughed to release it.

"I don't know, Boyd..."

"Or you could take me to the cave out by Mule Kick. That was the one we near got stuck in that time. Bet you'd know how to get us out of there this time. Right?"

Jackson wiped sweaty palms across his shirt. He shook his head.

"I bet we could even go all the way in the one down by the lake, you know, the one Dad made us promise never to try without him? 'Cause it went too far back and we could get lost?"

Just the thought of it made Jackson lightheaded.

"I need to sit down a minute." He walked out and rested against the seat of the mower.

"You need some water?" Boyd grabbed the thermos and handed it to Jackson.

"Thanks Bud," he said and then took a few gulps. Sweat dripped from his nose. "What is wrong with me?" He wondered.

Boyd shrugged. "Maybe you don't want to take me."

The last thing Jackson wanted to do was make Boyd feel bad, once again.

"That's not it."

"Well, Dad didn't want to take me anymore. Maybe you don't too. Maybe you think I can't do it."

"No, Boyd, I swear..."

"Dad was afraid I'd get you killed or somethin'."

"That's not true."

Boyd nodded furiously. "I heard him tell Ma one time."

Jackson's shoulders slumped forward. "I'm sorry, Bud. That wasn't fair of him."

"You think he was right."

Jackson took Boyd by the shoulder. "No, I don't, Boyd. I know you can do it. You'd just have to take it slow."

Boyd perked up. "So, you'll take me?"

Jackson swallowed hard and nodded. "I'll try. We'll try to work something out."

Boyd leapt into the air, his usual response to getting his way. Jackson wondered how he was going to make good on his word when he had no intention of ever stepping foot into another cave again.

BOYD'S PLAN

15

All day long Boyd asked Jackson for the time even though he was wearing the watch Papaw gave him for his 16th birthday.

"I thought you knew how to tell time," Jackson reminded him as he unloaded heavy bags of corn from the delivery truck parked at the mill's receiving door.

Boyd nodded. "I want to be sure," he said, rocking on his heels with too much force, causing himself to wobble.

"It's 2:30, Boyd. I know you're excited about Lindsey coming over, but you seem more neurotic than usual. What's up?"

Boyd's face went full red, concealing the patches of freckles there.

"'Cause of this." He held out an open hand. In it was a ring.

Jackson looked closer, then asked if he could pick it up.

"Sure," gushed Boyd. "It's a wedding ring."

"A what?" Jackson took it from his brother and inspected it.

Clearly one of Boyd's finds. It was encrusted with dirt, but it looked to be a gold band, highlighted by a red stone. He wondered if it was one of the "treasures" Boyd had snuck out of the shed before the big clean up.

"It's a wedding ring. I'm gonna 'prose to Lindsey. She likes red."

Jackson held up his hand, for several reasons. One, to stop the thought of Boyd being married to anyone from creeping into his brain, and two, to keep Boyd in check.

"You're going to give Lindsey a ring covered in dirt? Don't you think you should wash it first? And who does it belong to, anyway? Where did you find it?"

Boyd took it back and looked at it. "I guess I can clean it some," he admitted.

"Some? Yeah, maybe a lot. Where'd you find it?" Jackson asked again.

"In the field," Boyd threw his arm toward the horse pasture. "I was digging for worms near the pond."

"Better have Ma look at it," Jackson suggested. "Might be something she's lost and you wouldn't want to give away something she'll want back."

The best thing was to let Ma handle the whole situation, wedding plans and all. Jackson had heard Boyd talk of marrying Lindsey on several occasions, but it had always been met with a change of subject or lack of seriousness. He had never known there to be a ring involved before.

Boyd ran off to find Ma. It wasn't long before curiosity overtook Jackson and he followed suit, even though he had promised Natalie he would stay out of the shop.

"Ma says it's a ruby!" Boyd bounced over to Jackson as he entered the shop and then bounced back to his mother.

"Really?" Jackson asked. Avoiding Natalie's glare, he stared directly at Ma.

She was busy cleaning the dirt off with a toothbrush. "I said it 'looks like' a ruby. I can't be sure, but the ring is marked 14 karat. Could be pretty old. That pond was dug back before Papaw's time. Maybe one of your ancestors dropped it there while they were digging it out."

"From back then? You think the women folk were out there helping dig the pond by hand?" Jackson said it half-jokingly, not imagining women in long skirts and petty coats removing the wheelbarrows of dirt it would have taken to excavate the half-acre pond.

"Are you saying they weren't capable?" Natalie asked him.

"No, that's not it. Not incapable. I-I guess I just don't picture them doing that kind of heavy work."

Natalie clucked her tongue in annoyance and walked away. "Figures," she said.

"Who do you think built this place?" asked Ma.

Jackson wished he had stayed in the granary.

"We know your ancestors didn't have slaves, which meant every hand available did the labor," she explained. "The women, the children, whoever was around. I thought Papaw taught you all the Hawking history."

Jackson shook his head. "Most of his stories were about manly stuff. I don't think he was very progressive where women were concerned."

"Apples and trees," came Natalie's voice from behind one of the shelves.

Ma grinned at Jackson's expense, which annoyed him.

"Very funny. I guess now I'm a caveman. Haha, get it? So, what's the deal on the ring? Are you going to let him give it to Lindsey? You know he intends to ask her to marry him with it."

Boyd had been standing in one place, bobbing up and down for the last few minutes. He too, wanted an answer to that question.

"Well, I would like to have it looked at, Boyd, if it's okay with you. Not that I don't think Lindsey is deserving of such a beautiful ring, but we should know its history, don't you think?"

"Yeah, I guess," Boyd said and stopped bobbing.

"And I also think we should talk to Joy first before you go off proposing to her daughter, don't you also think?"

This time he shrugged his shoulders.

"It would be the proper thing to do, son."

Boyd let out a big sigh. "Okay."

"I do have a temporary solution for you, though. You can pick any one of those rings from the tray over there and give it to Lindsey as a promise ring. Will that suit your purpose?"

Ma was referring to the silver and turquoise rings displayed in the jewelry case. Boyd often admired them. He picked out the one with the largest stone and headed happily toward the house to wait for his girl.

"Nice bait and switch, Ma," Jackson said when he was gone.

"Just a detour, really," she explained. "You know the conversation is sure to come back around. Sooner or later I'll have to have an answer for him."

Jackson shook his head. "For all our sakes, hopefully later."

LIKE BLOOD FROM A GORE HOLE

16

It wasn't long before the familiar blue SUV drove up. Jackson was outside the mill and waved to Joy as she stopped to say hello.

"Hey, ladies," he said, peering into the window. "He's up at the house waiting for you, Sassafrass."

"You mean!" Lindsey complained with a grin.

"Okay, you two. Don't start. I'm supposed to be helping at church tonight and I'm running late."

"Okay, well, when you have time later, you may want to talk to Ma about Boyd's big idea," Jackson said with a wink.

"What kind of idea?" Joy wanted to know.

He didn't want to give it away in front of Lindsey, so he held his hand below Lindsey's line of view and pointed to his ring finger. "It has something to do with popping a question."

Joy nodded. "I knew this was coming. That's why she's on birth control. My kids are all grown and I'm in no mood to raise any more babies."

Jackson chuckled. "Well, that's more than I ever wanted to think about, so I'll let you and Ma deal with that. I just thought I'd fill you in. He's already found the circle thing, understand?"

"Thanks for the warning," she said. "Tell your mother I hope to see her later."

"Will do. And good luck."

Jackson bent down to look in at Lindsey. She responded by sticking her tongue at him. He returned the gesture.

"I swear, the two of you are toddlers," Joy lamented before heading over the bridge.

Jackson went back to work, arranging the sacks of grain he'd need for the next day's grind closer to the elevator. He thought about Boyd's plan to marry Lindsey, picturing him getting down on one knee to 'pose to her. Then he thought about the day he had made a similar proposal to Natalie, as part of a conversation they were having and not an "official" proposal. They had talked about what they each wanted out of a future together, but he never got the chance to make it official. All the conversations they'd had about marriage and babies and building their own home on the family land washed away in an instant.

As he worked, Jackson struggled to push out unwelcome thoughts the way a novice would in meditation, trying and failing and then repeating the process. A glance at the knives hanging in a row above the inventory desk was all it took. The compulsion to pull the curved one from the wall and run it down his arm tightened his muscles and raised his heartrate.

Stop, he demanded of his wayward mind.

Maybe he could lose himself in the rhythm of the turbines, picking up and throwing on the pulse he felt through the floor. He'd done it a million times before, allowing his mind to zone out on nothingness while his body drove itself. This time he found it impossible.

Disparaging words from his father rattled his memory. Words about being a failure as a father and a husband slapped in measure with the serpentine belts. How much of what he said were the same words he'd heard from his own father? More shit rolling downhill? How many generations would be visited upon by this need to inflict pain on your own son? Of course Jackson would be a horrible father if he continued this tradition.

With every step down into the quagmire of familial shortcomings, the velocity with which Jackson threw each sack down grew. One sack hit the corner of a wooden post and split open. It was fascinating to watch the grain spill out like blood from a gore hole. The shhhhhh of the kernels sliding against each other and puddling on the ground below soothed him somehow. He lifted another sack and threw it against the post with similar results. More "blood" spilled. More gratification from the sight of it. It didn't matter that grain was being wasted, or what a pain in the ass it would be to clean up. The hulls and dust released into the air stuck to his sweat, caked on his skin, settled in his hair. He didn't care. It felt good to not give a shit and he had no intention of stopping. He threw another.

A siren in the distance broke through the indulgence of the melee. Not the tornado siren. A fire truck or an ambulance.

Where could they possibly be headed? They had to be coming his direction, there was no other house nearby.

Ma, he thought, and immediately ran around to the shop.

Ma and Natalie were busy with their last customer, closing up for the day. They turned as Jackson charged into the shop, their faces changing when they saw his.

"What's wrong?" Ma asked. "Why are you covered – "

"You don't you hear it?"

He realized the sounds from the machinery kept them from hearing the siren.

And there it was, getting louder by the second. Right at the bottom of the hill.

Jackson ran outside, his mother, Natalie, and their customer right behind him.

An ambulance followed by a fire truck approached the parking lot entrance, going by it on the gravel road, meaning they were headed across the bridge.

His heart racing, Jackson ran toward them, reaching the fire truck and calling to the driver.

"John! What's going on?"

The driver stopped the vehicle as the ambulance drove on.

"Jackson!" he yelled back. "We got a call from the house, something unintelligible. They thought it might be your mom in trouble. But, there she is, so it couldn't be her."

"Lindsey," said Natalie. "It might be Lindsey who called."

They looked up toward the house across the river and saw Lindsey on the bluff, waving her arms and approaching the ambulance.

Jackson ran across the bridge ahead of the fire truck. Ma and Natalie got into Natalie's car and followed.

As Jackson got to Lindsey, he noticed her clutching her chest. He worried she might be having a heart attack.

"Boyd," she said with very little breath. "Boyd fell."

Jackson looked around.

"Where? Where is he, Lindsey? In the house?"

"Dead." She pointed toward the horse pasture.

Jackson felt himself wobble. "What do you mean, dead? Boyd's not dead."

Lindsey grabbed her chest with one hand and pointed again with the other. "Dead." She said breathlessly. Then she waved toward the field. "Dead stones."

"The cemetery," Natalie said, catching up. "Do you mean the cemetery, Lindsey?"

Lindsey nodded and then doubled over. Natalie grabbed her as Jackson told the ambulance driver where to go.

"Just follow the fence line and there's a dirt road to the left. Follow that and you can't miss it."

As Natalie helped Lindsey into her car, Jackson jumped behind the wheel and told her to get in. He took off before her door was closed and sped around the fire truck first and then the ambulance, leading them to the spot where he thought his brother might be lying. Hopefully not dead.

He saw no sign of Boyd in the cemetery.

"Where?" he asked Lindsey.

From the back seat, upset and crying, Lindsey pointed past the cemetery, to the tree line and the gully beyond it. Jackson imagined Boyd lying at the bottom of the gully, broken and lifeless.

"Please, Lord, don't let him be dead," he said as he opened the car door. "In the gully!" he yelled to the ambulance crew.

As the rescuers got out and grabbed their equipment, Jackson walked around the far side of the car.

"Ma, I think you should just stay here. You won't be able to walk past the cemetery wall anyway." He opened Lindsey's door.

"Be gentle with her, she's very upset," Natalie prompted him.

Jackson stepped back and allowed Natalie to help Lindsey from the car, realizing his sense of urgency might frighten her into non-cooperation. He'd seen it happen many times with Boyd. The harder you press, the more he shut down. They needed her to lead them to Boyd. There was no time for games. In fact, he began to worry about how much time had passed since hearing the initial siren in the distance. How long had it been since Lindsey made the phone call? And how long had it taken her to run from the gully to the house to make the call in the first place? His anxiety level rose to the point of panic.

Natalie, on the other hand, spoke to Lindsey in quiet tones, calming her and letting her lead them toward the tree line. As soon as they stepped past the first row of trees the land dropped off into a rocky slope which fell about twenty feet, then bottomed out with a small stream which fed the river beyond it. Scattered about were downed branches and wild grape vines hanging from the trees. Only then could they hear the horrible screaming.

There, lying about halfway up from the stream on the other side of the ravine was Boyd, his right leg lying in an unnatural position, his left leg pinned under him. He was howling like an animal stuck in a trap.

The howling was a good sign. At least he wasn't dead.

The fact that he didn't stop howling the whole time the ambulance crew tried to ready him for the climb back out began to unnerve Jackson.

Granted, the bone in his right leg was protruding from his thigh, clear through his jeans, and was a good enough reason for anyone to be screaming in pain. Jackson couldn't understand how the crew stayed so calm throughout the whole rescue. Shutting off the blood supply to the wound, splinting what they could and then sliding him onto a board before lifting him into a basket, all done quickly and with very little communication between the crew. Then there was the climb back up the hill. It took ropes and several slides backward in the mud before it was accomplished. Even with all the blood he must have lost, which should have worn him out, Boyd still managed to holler the whole time.

Jackson tried to calm him, taking his hand and assuring him it would be okay, but Boyd wasn't having it and continued to howl.

"I don't know how you do it," Jackson commented to one of the crew as they lifted him, still howling, into the ambulance.

He could have been talking about the carnage, or the where-with-all it took to stay focused under life and death situations, or the strength it took to carry someone Boyd's size up a rocky incline like that, but the paramedic knew exactly what Jackson meant when he asked the question.

Without skipping a beat, the guy answered, "Honestly, I don't even hear it."

Maybe it was the helplessness he felt which unnerved him. His brother was calling out for help, unable to handle the pain. Once again, Jackson was powerless to do anything of value for someone he loved in a crisis situation. How had this become the recurring theme of his life? He was useless.

* * *

Before they ever moved him, the paramedics called in the helicopter to airlift Boyd to the hospital. Jackson's first reaction was to go along in the helicopter, but it was Ma's place to do so. She would be the one to make medical decisions for him.

"Have you ever flown in a helicopter, Mrs. Hawking?" the paramedic asked as the helicopter approached the field.

"Can't be any worse than being on a tractor with your father," she said to Jackson, a slight shake in her voice.

"Other than you'll be a couple hundred feet higher, it will be exactly like that."

Natalie took her hand. "You'll be fine, Ruth. They know what they're doing."

She looked at the paramedic. "If it's going to help my son, then I'm ready."

Once Boyd was loaded into the chopper, Jackson jumped back into the driver's seat of Natalie's car.

"And what do you think you're doing?" Natalie stood at the door.

"Get in, we need to go," Jackson ordered her.

"You're forgetting something. First of all, this is my car. And second, if the way you drove from the house to here is any indication of how you're going to drive out on that windy-ass road into town, all I have to say is no freakin' way. You'll kill us all."

"Fine. You drive," he grouched and climbed over to the passenger seat. "Let's go."

Natalie got in and looked to the back seat.

"You okay?" she asked Lindsey, who had become very quiet. "I called your mom and she's going to meet us at the hospital."

"Go home," Lindsey said with a pout.

Natalie turned to Jackson.

"You should sit with her. She's shaking."

Jackson gave an impatient eye roll, but realized she was right. He sighed, got out and moved into the back seat with Lindsey, reluctantly taking her hand. On her finger was the turquoise ring Boyd had chosen for her. Jackson tried to reassure her that everything would be fine even though he doubted it would be. Boyd looked pretty bad. His face was pale and his legs were so broken. It was hard to tell how much blood he'd lost with all the leaves and rocks lying beneath him, but his jeans were pretty soaked with it. Just the thought of it made his stomach twist.

"Ow," Lindsey said and pulled her hand from his.

"Sorry." Jackson hadn't realized how hard he was squeezing as his thoughts took him to dark places.

He finally sat back and allowed the roll of the hills as well as the blur of trees going by to lull him into a hypnotic state, taking notice of their location only when they reached the first stoplight before town. Looking down, he saw Lindsey's hand on his, patting his skin in gentle encouragement. He leaned over and gave her a kiss on the forehead. It was an act which would, in normal circumstances be met with resistance, but today was met with a slight smile.

When they got to the hospital, Ma was huddled in the waiting room with Joy, who immediately ran to her daughter and held on fast.

"Thank God you're alright," she said.

"Go home," Lindsey sobbed into her mother's chest.

"They've taken him up to surgery," Ma announced. "There's a waiting room nearby they said we can go to."

Jackson nodded.

"I'm going to take her home," said Joy. "I think she's had all she can handle for one day."

"I agree," Jackson told her. "We'll call you with any news."

Then he looked at Lindsey, still engulfed in her mother's arms. He mouthed the words "Thank you", and thought, *Thank you for saving my brother's life. Thank you for comforting me when I should have been comforting you.*

THE HARDEST PART

17

The walk to the surgical waiting room was a slow one, with Ma using Jackson's arm as well as her cane to plod along. It seemed to be taking more effort than usual for her to drag her left foot forward. *She must be exhausted.* After all, she'd worked a full day before any of this even happened.

With each pained step, she began talking about the helicopter ride.

"They lost his pulse twice while we were up in the air and had to shock him twice with those paddle things. It can't be good, you know. They said he lost a lot of blood." She seemed so calm talking about it at first, but then she stopped walking and began to cry. "Why am I losing all of the men in my life? What am I going to do without my son?"

Jackson pulled her to him to reassure her. She said "son" singularly, but he knew she meant him, too. He'd been unwilling to make any real commitment to stay put and now Boyd could be dying on the operating table as they spoke. None of the men in his mother's life were very reliable, it seemed.

"I'm here, Ma. I'm not going anywhere and neither is Boyd. With all the technology they have now, titanium parts and all, they're going to fix him up and he'll be fine. As good and goofy as new. You got that?"

"He's right, Ruth," added Natalie. "We have to be positive and send positive thoughts. It does no good to think the worst. Have faith in God and the doctors He's put here for Boyd. They both know what they're doing."

Ruth leaned over to Natalie and patted her arm, then pulled away from Jackson.

"What is all over you, anyway?" she asked, dusting herself off.

In the excitement, Jackson had forgotten about the mess in the mill and the evidence sticking to him.

"Just some dust. One of the grain sacks broke open," he explained.

Ma looked him over, and accepting his explanation, reached for the nearest waiting room chair. Natalie offered Jackson the seat next to his mother, but he was in no condition to sit still. He shook his head and motioned for her to take it.

"I need to find a bathroom. Anybody want anything from the vending machines?"

* * *

After washing off in the men's room, he brought two "gourmet coffees" to his mother and Natalie but they hardly acknowledged his gesture before resuming their conversation. *Praying*, he thought, although it was hard to tell. There was barely more than a whisper between them.

He stepped back away from them, still reeling from the day's events, watching Natalie as she placed her coffee on the floor next to her chair. She took Ma's free hand and closed her eyes in meditation. She was praying with the confidence only someone with strong faith can know, yet exposing her doubts in the tautness of her jawline and the uncontrollable shaking of her foot against the metal leg of the waiting room chair. And of course, fidgeting with the hem of her t-shirt. Was Natalie having doubts about God's ability to fix things? Could there be a chip in her "perfectly perfect" porcelain exterior after all?

Whatever was going through her mind, she was stunning. Dad was right. Every good and wonderful thing about her made Jackson that much more aware of his own failings. Since his return, every moment spent with her had been verification of his inability to pull his shit together. The very reason he needed to keep as far away from her as possible. Besides, he should be making his own thoughtful petition to God, asking Him to spare his brother's life.

"I'm going to find the chapel," he announced. "Let me know if anyone comes to talk to you."

He walked off without a response from either of them. Did they even hear him? Had he become invisible?

Doesn't matter, he thought. *It's not as if they need me.*

He found the small, quiet chapel not far from the waiting room. It was a modern wood and glass construct which projected out of the bare, flat hospital walls. The tall windows allowed natural light and nature to fill the room and calm the soul.

He found a seat and decided to kneel. Bringing his hands together to pray, he rested his forehead on them, eyes closed.

"I don't know what to say, Lord. Please don't let my brother die? And if you let him live, please don't let him be crippled for the rest of his life. Not that what I say matters, you're going to do whatever you want anyway. It's really all up to you. So you decide. We'll deal with the consequences. At least give us the strength for whatever's coming. If you aren't going to make him better, then at least help us get through it. And him. Help him through this, Lord. He doesn't have much patience for being sick or hurt. He's just a kid. Well, maybe not in years, but in maturity. He doesn't deserve any of this and neither does Ma. Please watch over her, too." With a sigh, he added, "I don't know what else to say." His mind went blank. God was going to do whatever He wanted to anyway. Everyone insisted He had a plan, right? What if Jackson petitioned for something totally against God's plan? Then his prayers would serve for nothing. So what could he say to make a difference? He struggled to answer that question. He struggled to understand what the question even was. He grasped for words and hoped God would untangle the chaos in his mind.

IF ONLY TARZAN HAD WINGS

18

Jackson was so absorbed in the thoughts taking him in fifty separate directions, he didn't hear the chapel door open or the seat next to him creak when someone sat down. He did feel her presence, though. Warmth, followed by steady breathing.

"Any news?" he asked.

"One of the surgeons came in and spoke to your mother. She said it was touch and go, but they finally got Boyd stable. Her job's done, I guess, so now the orthopedic surgeon is working on him. He's going to have at least one pin in his leg and another in his ankle. It could be another hour or two for all that to happen. She said there's a lot of damage."

Jackson nodded. "Thanks."

Natalie got up to go.

"This is exactly what he talked about," he said absently.

"What is?" she asked, sitting back down.

"All the calamities. One after the other. Ripping your heart out. Bringing you to your knees. Some kind of punishment for some past wrongdoing. I've had enough of it. As soon as we get Boyd situated I'm taking them both and moving them out of here. Someone else can deal with this bullshit. Maybe they'll have better luck."

"You're only saying those things because you're upset."

"Damn right I'm upset!" He raised his voice and then retreated when he saw the red in Natalie's cheeks. "Sorry."

"You have every right to be shaken, Jackson, but I don't think your thoughts are clear right now. Your family isn't being punished for any wrongdoing. These are things that happen to other people too. People get sick. They have accidents, and sometimes they die. Not because God or some unseen force is punishing them, but because life happens and it isn't always fair. Selling the mill and moving away isn't going to cure your mother's illness any more than it'll take away Boyd's talent for getting himself in trouble. Your father was wrong to put the inevitability of these things in your head."

"Maybe," said Jackson, if only to appease her. So far, his father had been right about a lot of things. He'd been right about Natalie, about the way she would make him feel. He was right about the steady stream of disasters giving him nightmares. Jackson was trudging through one of those nightmares now, feeling useless and afraid. Exactly what his father said he'd be. "And then, maybe not. Either way, I'm done," he said as he stood up to leave.

As he walked out of the chapel, he thought she might follow him to argue her point further, maybe hoped she would, but it was some time before she rejoined him and Ma in the waiting room.

"What's wrong?" Ma asked when Natalie finally came in and sat in a different set of chairs away from them.

Natalie shook her head, unwilling to give an answer, but Jackson noticed the puffiness under her eyes, the red outline around her nose. She'd been crying. Hard. For him?

Don't waste your tears, he thought.

* * *

An hour and a half later, as Ma lay sleeping against Jackson's shoulder, a doctor entered the waiting room. He explained what it took to fix Boyd's fractured left leg and insert the pins now holding it together. He told them about the shattered right ankle, and how it, too, needed pins to hold the bones together and would probably give him trouble for a good long while. He talked about the surgeon who saved Boyd's life more than once on the operating table and what a great job she did. Then he said Boyd was in recovery, and once they had him awake, they'd be able to see him for a minute before he'd be taken up to his room.

Ma grabbed the surgeon's hand and thanked him.

"Bless you," she said. "Bless you and the other doctors for saving my son's life."

"Yes, ma'am," the doctor nodded. "We do what we can, and for that, we can always use more blessings."

* * *

Boyd's eyes fluttered open for a moment as they arrived in the recovery room. He looked around, then closed them.

"Boyd," the nurse called to him. "Look who's here."

This time when his eyes opened, they locked on his mother.

"Am I dead?" he asked with a thick, raspy voice.

Ma gave a teary laugh. "No, you're not dead, son, you're in the hospital."

The nurse handed him a cup of ice chips and instructed him to suck on them.

"I was flying."

"That's right, Buddy," said Jackson. "You flew in the helicopter."

"Ah-uh-uh-uh-ah-uh-uhuhahh," sang Boyd.

Ma looked at Jackson, who shrugged his shoulders.

"He's drugged up. Who knows what weird stuff might come out of his mouth?"

"I'm Tarzan," he mumbled, his mouth full of ice chips.

"Okay," Jackson nodded. "You be Tarzan. I'll be Jane."

"No," Boyd insisted, his head jerking and falling side to side. "Lindsey is Jane."

Ma tried to catch the ice chips falling from his mouth and almost lost her balance.

"Okay, then," said Jackson as he held on to his mother. "We'll talk about that later. Suck on your ice."

* * *

Once Boyd was situated in his room, the truth of his accident was revealed. He explained how he really had been playing Tarzan to Lindsey's Jane when he attempted to swing across the ravine using a wild grape vine. His intention was to carry her across with him. If Lindsey hadn't had the presence of mind not to let him, she would have ended up with similar injuries, or worse.

"I was showing her it was safe," explained Boyd. "But the vine didn't stay up in the tree like it was s'posed to and I fell. Then she left me and I was all by myself and it hurt so bad."

"Serves you right, it hurt!" Ma had apparently gotten past the worried stage of the incident and moved on to reproach. "You could be dead right now! What a foolish thing to do, Boyd! And to put Lindsey's life in danger, too! That poor girl is traumatized by what happened today and it's all your fault."

"Ma," Jackson touched her arm. *The guy was barely back in the land of the living.*

"I know I shouldn't upset him, but I want him to know how his actions affect other people. I want him to know how close we came to losing him so he never does anything so reckless again. Do you understand that?" she asked Boyd.

Boyd mustered the sorriest face he could and apologized.

"Sorry, Ma. I'm tired."

As Jackson had seen on many occasions, Ma could go from pouncing lioness to purring kitten in no time flat. She nodded her approval and touched the hair on Boyd's forehead, gently pushing his curls to one side. He followed her hand with his eyes and in an instant he was asleep, as if she had turned off the lights with her reassuring gesture.

Then she turned to Jackson, her face suddenly pale, her unsteady hand shaking the cane held in it.

"I need to go home and get to bed."

She had pushed herself as far as her body could take her.

FAILURE ABOUNDS

19

When Ma wasn't up by nine the next morning, Jackson began to worry. He'd planned on letting her sleep in after such a long night, but he knew she'd want to be with Boyd at the hospital. He wasn't sure whether it was worse to let her sleep too long or to wake her too early.

He thought if he made coffee and bacon, the smell of breakfast would wake her. When it didn't, he thought, *I'll give her 'til ten,* and then cleaned up the kitchen.

He called Gary, Boyd's helper in the mill, to tell him what happened and let him know that the mill would be closed, possibly for a few days. He knew Natalie would be meeting them at the hospital later. She and Ma could decide what to do about the mill then.

As he waited for Ma to wake up, an uneasiness persisted. He paced the house, waiting for ten o'clock, his self-imposed deadline weighing heavily upon him.

As soon as the clock hit ten he went to his mother's room, flicked the light switch and called her name. She wasn't in her bed.

Good, she's in the bathroom.

He noticed her bathroom door was open and as he turned to give her privacy, he realized her feet were protruding from the doorway.

"Ma?" he called and rushed to her.

She was lying on her side in front of the sink.

He knelt beside her. "Ma, what happened?"

"Fell," she mumbled.

"Is anything broken?" He was afraid to move her in case there was.

"Can't feel," she mumbled. Her lips barely moved.

Jackson ran for his phone and called 911.

"Natalie," she mumbled when he was done.

"You want me to have her meet us?"

"No," she seemed frustrated. "Here."

What was the point? By the time she got there they might be gone, but he did what Ma asked and called. Natalie, of course, didn't hesitate to say she was on her way.

The paramedics arrived and looked Ma over. She was in a lot of pain and they were afraid she'd broken her hip. Jackson was glad he hadn't moved her. But it wasn't just the hip they were concerned with. It was the paralysis. Ma was unable to move her extremities and spoke out of one side of her mouth. A stroke was possible, but more likely she was having a relapse – a setback of severe symptoms some MS patients experience from time to time. She apparently had lain there for hours, powerless to get up or call out for Jackson.

Natalie arrived as they were getting into the ambulance. Ma insisted on talking to her.

She leaned in as Ma gave her instructions, to what, Jackson had no idea, but as they left in the ambulance Natalie stayed at the house, saying she'd see them in a bit.

* * *

Natalie caught up with Jackson while Ma was out of the room having an MRI done. It gave him the chance to ask what the big secret was.

"Don't tell her I told you. She'll be mortified. She asked me to strip the bed and wash everything."

Jackson considered the depth of his mother's embarrassment. Losing control of her muscles meant losing control of her bladder, too. She wouldn't have wanted Jackson to know she wet the bed.

"Thank you," he said. Even though his mind went back and forth between being glad Natalie was there and resenting her for it, he couldn't help but be grateful for the trust Ma put in her and how she consistently stepped up to the task. It was reassuring and infuriating at the same time.

"Really, it's no problem, Jackson. I love your mother. I would do anything for her."

He nodded in agreement. "I know. I just wanted to make sure you knew..." Thinking of his mother laying there in pain while he wasted time fidgeting around the house irritated him. When was he going to get his shit together? Why couldn't he be there for the people he loved and ever just do the right thing for them? Afraid to let her see his emotion, he turned away to take control. "I want you to know it's appreciated, that's all. Not just for today, but for every day you've been here for them."

Natalie opened her mouth to speak and then appeared to think better of it before finally accepting his thanks. "You're very welcome," she said.

"I should have gone in to wake her sooner," he said. "Lord knows how long she was laying there."

Natalie touched his arm. "I would have figured she was still sleeping as well. Don't beat yourself up over it."

Too late for that. "What if she thought she was going to die and that I'd abandoned her? You heard her last night. The men in her life suck."

"That wasn't what she said, Jackson."

"No, she said we were unreliable. Same thing."

"She's afraid of losing you. If y'all sucked so much, she wouldn't care."

"Yeah? Well, maybe she shouldn't care so much. Maybe we don't deserve her love. Maybe she'd be better off without us. I'm sure there are other men out there who are more worthy."

Natalie gave a tilt of the head and a raised eyebrow. "Are we still talking about your mother?"

Jackson felt his cheeks go hot and shifted in his seat. *Why did she always have to be like this?*

GOING DOWN?

20

Jackson fled judgment in the Emergency Room and rode the elevator up to Boyd's floor, thinking Boyd would probably be upset by the lack of visitors the day after his near death experience. He had no idea what was going on with Ma yet.

Opening the door to Boyd's room, Jackson realized he hadn't brought his brother anything. Not even a puzzle book.

He stepped inside the room and stopped. Confusion washed over him. There was a young girl in scrubs pulling all the sheets off Boyd's bed and stuffing them into a large, bagged container. The rest of the room was stripped clean of anything related to Boyd. No hanging IV bag, nothing on the tray table to show he'd been there.

"Where's my brother?" he asked.

The girl was startled. "You'll have to check with the nurse," she said. "I just clean."

He backed out and found the nurse's station. There were a few people buzzing around it, doing their best to ignore him.

"Excuse me," he said. "Can someone tell me what happened to my brother? He was in that room last night."

One of the nurses looked up from her computer screen. "Hawking?"

"Yes."

"Are you a relative?"

"Yes." Jackson stayed his instinct to worry. "I'm his brother."

"He's been moved to ICU."

"ICU? For what? What happened?"

The nurse shrugged. "Sorry, I don't have that information, you'll have to contact his doctor."

"I don't even know who his doctor is," Jackson realized. "He had emergency surgery last night and was brought up here."

The nurse typed something onto her keyboard. "Dr. Allen is his attending. You can ask for him up at the ICU desk. Next floor."

"Thanks," he said and walked to the elevator. In a daze he pushed the button, then imagined the doors opening. Before him no elevator waited expectantly, there was only a deep pit of cement, iron girders and high-voltage wires in its place. He jumped and disconnected a live wire, electrocuting himself. Dead before hitting the bottom. He saw it clearly. His heart thumped out of rhythm, squeezing in on itself until the tightness took his breath away.

The doors opened, reality returned. With sweaty palms, he got in and rode it to the next floor where he followed signs to the ICU. There was a sign-in sheet and instructions. Visitation was for family members only, two at a time, for a fifteen minute period at the top of each hour. That meant a ten minute wait until the next period. A ten minute wait to calm his ass down and convince himself he wasn't insane.

He began a text to Natalie, to tell her what was going on with Boyd and give his shaking hands something to do, but then he thought she might let it slip to Ma where he was, and she didn't need that. He discarded the message.

Eight more minutes. *Forget about my sanity, what the hell was happening with his family?* Twenty-four hours ago they were talking about Boyd proposing to Lindsey. Now Ma was in serious trouble and Boyd was in the ICU. Was his brother going to leave this hospital alive?

Christ, where are you? These are good people who hurt no one. They do as you ask. They honor you and serve you, and this is what they get? Someone needs to explain this to me, 'cause I don't understand.

His fingers were weaved together, covering his bowed head when he heard the double doors to the ICU unlatch. Others had gathered at the door and sprinted in as soon as they were allowed. Fifteen minutes was not a very long time, and yet, it could be an eternity when you sat at the sick bed of someone you loved.

Jackson found his brother's open room. As he entered, the hiss-beat-beat of the respirator stopped him. He listened to the sound and watched Boyd's chest rise and fall. A machine to the right of him whirred as it pushed fluid through clear tubing.

What the hell was going on?

He slowly stepped up to the bed. Boyd lay sleeping amongst tubes and wires and hanging IV bags. It was hard to know what to do with all this, never mind what to say. He wanted Boyd to know he was there.

"Hey, Buddy. It's me. I'm here. Sorry it took so long, but I have a good excuse, I really do. Boyd?"

A nudge to the shoulder prompted no response, so he did it again. Still nothing.

Man, they must have him on the good stuff, 'cause he's really out of it.

"Boyd?"

A nurse appeared at the glass door. She walked away and then came back with a doctor.

The doctor came in and introduced himself as Dr. Allen.

Jackson explained who he was to Boyd.

Dr. Allen nodded. "We attempted contact with his mother, but no one could reach her."

Jackson thought about his mother's phone, probably still sitting on her bedside table.

"My mother is downstairs in the ER right now," he answered.

"Oh," said the doctor. "I'm sorry to hear that. Was she also involved in the fall?"

"No," Jackson answered. "She's having some sort of attack. Something to do with her Multiple Sclerosis."

"Oh," said the doctor again. "At least she's in very capable hands. Does this mean you'll be making medical decisions for Boyd?"

"I guess so, yeah," Jackson nodded, then got right to the point. "So, what's going on with my brother? What is all this stuff?"

"Right now we have him in a medically induced coma. This equipment is doing the heavy lifting for him while he rests. He'll be unable to communicate with you."

"A coma?" Jackson felt his body go hot.

"Medicinally induced. The coma is purposeful," he said, pointing to the wires and tubes, "to give his body a chance to heal. We thought it best after his temperature spiked early this morning, which indicated an infection. A round of stronger antibiotics was tried downstairs, but before the antibiotic had a chance to work, he had a seizure."

"He had a seizure this morning? We didn't know."

"Yes, well, the seizure caused some concern, you know he's had such a rough time already. That's when we were called in. The team agreed it was best to transfer him to the ICU and start the meds to induce a coma state. Up here he has constant supervision. There haven't been any other seizures, which is good news, but his temp is still higher than we'd like. We're keeping an eye on it."

"Okay, well, I guess you know what's best." Jackson struggled to keep his brain clear. He couldn't help but stare at all the machinery.

Ask questions, idiot. "So, what if his temperature doesn't go down? What happens then? You can die from an infection, right? What if this doesn't work? Is there another medicine you can try?"

The doctor sighed and looked Jackson straight in the eye. "A different medicine is one possibility. Infections can be stubborn and sometimes it takes a while to find the right meds to fight it with. But I don't want to give you false hope. I assume you're aware of the condition he was found in. Rocks and dirt and all kinds of bacteria had access not only to his open wound, but also a major artery. The surgeons did a great job with the debridement, cleaning out what they could, but I'm afraid if we can't get the infection under control, we may have to consider taking the leg."

Smack. Jackson's head snapped back and then felt himself go cold from his legs upward into his belly. Darkness came in from the sides. He willed himself to push it out, but the darkness grew stronger.

"Are you all right? You might want to sit here."

He heard the nurse drag a chair into position behind him, holding his arm as he sat.

Feeling foolish, he waited while his vision slowly cleared. Then, he apologized to the doctor.

"Sorry, that's never happened to me before."

"No worries. It's not uncommon. I'm sure this is all overwhelming for you."

"I have to tell you, Dr. Allen, the past two days have been a little more than I can deal with."

"It sounds as if it's been quite an episode."

The nurse appeared at the door, presenting Jackson with a juice box. He hadn't even seen her leave. He took it gladly.

"Thanks," he said.

"No problem," she answered.

The doctor had moved over to Boyd, checking the readouts coming from the machines. Once he seemed satisfied, he turned back toward Jackson.

"He's young and strong, both very positive indicators for healing and reasons to be hopeful. But for now, it's going to be more of a 'wait and see' situation, which can be very difficult on the family, I'm afraid. It's hard to have patience when you're worried about a loved one. Do you have any other questions for me?"

Jackson shook his head. He was having a hard time thinking. Questions would come later, when no one was around to ask.

"Well, I'll be here if you do. Just have the nurse come and find me."

Jackson nodded. When he felt normal enough, he got up and moved over to the bed, taking Boyd's hand. There he stood in quiet shock until a soft tone sounded the end of visitation. It was time to be go back to Ma now.

SO MUCH FOR BEDSIDE MANNERS

21

Just before he got to the door of his mother's room, Jackson stopped and tilted his head forward until he could see Natalie. He waved to get her attention and then beckoned her to come out.

"What's up? How's Boyd?" she asked.

The answer to her question gave him pause.

"What's wrong?"

Just say it.

"He's in the ICU," he said quietly.

"The ICU? What happened?"

Jackson pulled her further away from the door so Ruth wouldn't hear them.

"It's okay, she's asleep."

"I don't want to take the chance of her hearing any of this." He lowered his voice. "He's got an infection and it caused a seizure. They've got him in a coma now."

"He's in a coma?"

He nodded. "Medically induced. On purpose to give his body a chance to heal."

And they might cut off his leg. He thought it, but couldn't say it, even if he wanted to. He leaned back against the wall and looked up to the ceiling. "What am I going to tell her?"

Natalie shook her head. "Nothing. You tell her he's sore and tired but he's doing just fine. You can't put any more stress on her, Jackson. She's past her limit."

He nodded. "I can relate to that."

"Can I see him?" she asked.

"The sign says family only for fifteen minutes an hour."

Natalie looked away, her shoulders drooping. "Oh, I see."

Dick. He hadn't meant to hurt her feelings, the words just popped out. He could have taken it back or made a joke of it, but instead of saying something to make her feel better, he changed the subject.

"So what's going on with Ma? Has the doctor been in to see her yet?"

Lucky for him, she went with it.

"They took blood and a then someone came in to ask questions. I'm sure it will take a while now to get any answers. I guess we just wait."

"There's a lot of that going around." He should still apologize for hurting her feelings, but he couldn't force the words from his mouth. Apologizing would show he cared, and he couldn't.

A doctor came walking toward them, a tall man with a long face. He barely acknowledged either of them as he entered Ma's room.

"Mrs. Hawking?" he said loudly. "Mrs. Hawking?" As soon as her eyes opened, he said, "Dr. Bratton. I'm here to check your reflexes. Now tell me if you feel this." And with that, he pulled the blanket from her feet and ran a wooden stick up the arch of her foot. "Any feeling?" he asked.

Jackson stepped around him to stand at his mother's side. The doctor's abruptness unsettled him. He looked at Natalie, who had taken pointe opposite him. She rolled her eyes. Apparently, she too, was weirded out by the man.

Ma answered slowly, still groggy from sleep.

"Tingly. A little pain. Is it moving?" she asked.

He did the same procedure to her other foot.

"What about this one?"

"I felt something. Did it move?"

The doctor continued to ignore her question and pushed past Natalie to the head of the bed.

"I'm going to raise the bed so I can test your arms now."

He did as he said and then told her to hold her arms out. Wincing in pain, she could barely lift them.

He took one arm, held it up and then hit it with his little rubber hammer. Then he walked around to the other side, expecting Jackson to step out of the way without so much as a word of "excuse me". Again, he hit her arm with the little hammer.

"All right, Mrs. Hawking," he said after typing into the mobile computer. "What seems to be going on here is what's called an exacerbation. It's not uncommon in patients with MS to suffer an acute attack like this, especially if they've overexerted themselves, or had some sort of trauma preceding the episode."

"I see," said Ma.

Jackson offered an explanation. "My brother had an accident yesterday, and –"

"Then it would be fair to assume Mrs. Hawking has been under a great deal of stress?"

"Well, yes," Jackson answered. "She was up very late –"

"The way we treat these episodes is usually with a large dose of steroids, which may bring back some motion."

May? This guy was infuriating.

"Are you saying it might not work? What happens then?"

The doctor stared at him for a moment. "Yes, well, let's see how the steroids work first." Then he continued typing. Without another word, he left the room.

"What the hell was that?" Jackson asked when he was gone.

"Apparently, not all doctors are concerned with their bedside manner," Natalie chuckled as she straightened the blankets.

"Must know his stuff," was Ruth's mumbled reply.

A little later the ER doctor came in.

"Your x-rays show no breaks, Mrs. Hawking, but a bruised hip and some badly bruised ribs. No chips or sharp edges, so that's good. Nothing to puncture the lungs. Our biggest concern there is you being able to take deep breaths, so we're going to start the steroid treatment as soon as possible to keep the swelling down, and give you some ice packs to keep on those ribs. Our goals are a bit contrary to each other, what with trying to increase your mobility on the one hand and treating the injuries you incurred with immobilization on the other, but we'll take it one step at a time."

"The other doctor, the rude guy...," said Jackson.

"You mean Dr. Bratton?" The doctor asked with a smile.

"Yes, him. He said the steroids *may* help, which to me, means it's possible they may not. What happens if they don't?"

Boyd's doctor said they'd take his leg if the meds didn't work. Was there an equally horrible fate awaiting Ma?

"Well, why don't we just wait and see what happens with the steroid therapy?"

It was obvious to Jackson that no one wanted to talk about the next steps, which meant the next steps were bad news. Why wouldn't it be? He was so tired of hearing bad news his brain hurt.

ANOTHER CHIP IN THE PORCELAIN?

22

Jackson wasn't sure whether to stay with his mother in the ER or take advantage of the next fifteen minute ICU visitation with his brother.

"Maybe you should go see Boyd," he said to Natalie. "You go and visit him for a few minutes while I stay here with Ma."

"But, I'm not family," Natalie reminded him.

Before he could open his mouth to apologize for being such an asshole, Ma had a suggestion.

"Y'all go," she mumbled. "I'm not going anywhere, promise." With the little bit of power she had, she motioned toward the door.

They eyed one another and then agreed to it.

At the door to ICU there was a sign-in sheet. Jackson told Natalie to sign as Natalie Hawking.

"What should I put as my relationship to patient?" she asked. "Sister?"

"That'll work," Jackson answered. Blood was better than the other option.

* * *

Natalie went right to Boyd's bed, chirping, "Hey, Boyd," as if he weren't attached to machinery in a comatose state. "How's it going, Buddy?" She rubbed his arm as she looked him over. "Don't worry, Bud, you don't need to answer." Sizing up his situation, she said, "Well, you certainly win the prize for most tubes and wires connected to you, poor thing. We miss you, Big Guy. I hope you don't mind, Ma couldn't make it today, she was just too tired from staying up so late last night...I'm sure you understand. You'll just have to settle for me and your brother the caveman here." She paused, looking to Jackson.

"Hey, Boyd," said Jackson on cue. "It's me."

Leaning in toward Boyd's ear, she said, "I'd like to share some words with you, if it's all right."

Then she began a steady whisper, an inaudible prayer Jackson recognized by the movement of her lips. How did she manage to stay so calm, as close as she was to this poor, wrecked boy? It was all Jackson could do to keep himself from shaking like a twig in a storm. A storm which was threatening to swallow him whole.

He followed Natalie's lead and placed a hand on Boyd's arm, hoping his brother would somehow know his touch through the denseness of sleep. That's all it was, right? Sleep. He wasn't dead. For that Jackson should be grateful. He should thank someone for saving his brother's life. He wished he could be as sure as Natalie was in knowing who was responsible. Other than the doctors, anyway. And Lindsey's good sense.

"Do you really think it does any good?" He asked before he thought better of it.

"What?" she asked. "Prayer?"

He hadn't really meant to start the conversation. "Yeah, you know, 'The eyes of the Lord are on the righteous and his ears are attentive to their cry'." With a lift of his chin, he mused, "Wow, I can't believe I remember that." He nodded, proud of his recollection. Then he wagged his finger. "But then Daniel says, 'We do not make requests of you because we are righteous, but because of your great mercy.' His hands raised in question, he asked "So, which is it? Do we have to be righteous to ask, or is God merciful and will help every fool who asks? Do I even care, if my brother is saved in the end?"

"Of course you should care. Words are very powerful."

"And you think there's a God who is listening?"

"I believe –," she stopped, shaking her head. "This is very complicated stuff, Jackson. Are you sure you want to get into this right now?"

Jackson shook his head. He didn't. "No, it doesn't matter. I know you have faith. I know you still go to church and all."

"And what?" She asked with an injured tone. "Attending church defines my entire philosophy? Really? You know my whole belief system based on that one fact. Like that's all there is to it? Thanks for reducing me to a caricature."

"I didn't mean it as a bad thing. It's not like we never talked about stuff like this before."

She laughed. "And you think I haven't grown past the simplistic girl I once was, regurgitating everything Mom and Dad and Reverend Paulsen taught us? I've had a lot of time to discover myself while you were away, you know. I think you'd be surprised, Jackson. I can actually think for myself now."

"You always did think for yourself, Nat. That's not what I'm saying."

"It's what I'm saying, Jackson." She patted her chest. Then her eyes grew wide and bright, not with anger, but excitement. "I believe God is so much more than anything we can imagine; bigger, you know? Beyond our imagining." She became very animated, waving her arms in a circle. "Defining Him is-is like trying to catch wind in a jar. You can't do it. We try to make Him human, but He's not. I hate even referring to Him as Him, but for lack of a better defining quality..." Her voice calmed, "I think we feel His energy and His love, it's what flows through everything, and the angels and even Jesus, they're incarnations of Him, but so are we. It's like, He's the body and we're the cells and we're all connected by this energy, these synapses, if you will – the people and the animals and the trees and the rivers and all the universes – everything you can think of, and so when we pray - communication is so important, you know - it's like we send out a signal to The Brain that we need attention and then The Brain sends what we need to help us."

Oh boy. He closed his eyes and blew out a breath. "And then sometimes it doesn't," he replied. *Wasn't that obvious?*

"Well, maybe it doesn't always come in the form we expect. Sometimes it's in the form of a friend, or a teacher, or a doctor who can cure us," she said, pointing to Boyd. "And sometimes it's just a fleeting thought, or a notion in your head that leads you to an answer." She went back to rubbing Boyd's arm absentmindedly. "And then sometimes, there is no answer. We don't know what The Brain knows. We can't say what's best for the body as a whole. Only He can. Prayer is how we communicate with Him. It's our signal. Praying together, like in church, well, more voices just amplify the signal, you know, it ups the frequency of the vibration. Sometimes we pray to ask for help, and sometimes it's just to join in the rhythm of all the signals, to honor The Body and The Brain, to keep the signal flowing."

Jackson shook his head in wonder. "Wow."

"What? You think I'm crazy."

"No," he shook his head again. "I think I should stop making assumptions."

She smiled. "Just another opportunity for personal growth."

She was right about that and this time he was glad for it. Had he seen another chip in the assumed "perfect" porcelain? Maybe a crack? Maybe she was more human than he'd thought with her strange analogy of God and signals. And more beautiful in her obvious enthusiasm over it than he could allow himself to think.

REALITY CHECK

23

Back in Ma's room, a nurse came in to administer the steroid shot and something for her pain. Then she told them Ma would soon be admitted to her own room upstairs.

Later, Doctor Bratton came in to check on any success (or not) of the steroid shot. He did his tests, saying only what was necessary to Ma for instruction.

"Is your home equipped to support your mother's needs?" he asked to no one in particular.

"Pardon?" Jackson snapped to attention.

"Are you equipped for someone in your mother's condition? A power bed, possibly a lift?"

"Uh, no, I mean, I don't think so," Jackson replied.

"Hmm," said the neurologist, still making no eye contact. "Then a nursing home might be a more appropriate placement for you to consider. Do you have one in mind?"

"What are you saying?" asked Natalie.

"Well," he said, looking up from his keyboard toward some fixed point in the room about a foot off the bed. "I see very little improvement with the steroids given. Now, perhaps we can try a plasma exchange, but I'm not optimistic given the lack of results here. She'll need an abundance of care, which you seem ill equipped for. A nursing home would be the most suitable placement for her."

Jackson wanted to punch him.

Natalie must have sensed it because she shifted herself between them.

"Are you saying this is permanent?"

"It is a possibility, yes."

"How can that be? She was fine last night," Jackson argued.

"Fine? Are you sure, Mr. Hawking? Hasn't she been diagnosed with Multiple Sclerosis?"

"Well, yes, of course, but –"

"Then she wasn't fine. She suffers from a debilitating disease with varied symptoms. A setback like this is just one variant patients with MS are faced with. It is not an easy disease to live with, as I'm sure your mother can tell you. One day everything can seem relatively normal and the next day you can be lying in the ER talking to me."

Jackson wanted to lash out at the guy, but as infuriating as he might be, the doctor was not the enemy. Now was the time to put his faith in these professionals. What choice did he have? But a nursing home? Not if he could help it. There had to be another way.

After the doctor left, a nurse and other staff came in and transferred his mother to a portable bed in order to move her to an actual hospital room. Jackson noted that they didn't pick her up the way he would have, no, they had one person on either side of the bed and counted down before pulling on the sheets to move her over. Not lovingly, but safely. For her, yes, but also for themselves. Procedures put in place to protect their backs from injury. Jackson would have scooped her up in his arms and laid her down gently.

He and Natalie followed along as she was transported to her new room. Two nurses came in and hooked her up to monitors, introducing themselves and preparing her for an overnight stay.

This is what her life would be now. Strangers treating her like another task within their work day. Feeding her. Changing her clothes, her sheets; her diaper? Caring for her, yes, but caring about her? He shook his head in disbelief. This could not be what God intended. Not for Ma.

"You okay?" Natalie asked, her hand on his arm.

He looked at her hand so warmly placed and then at her.

"Yeah. Just tired."

"So sit down for a while. Close your eyes. She's sleeping now. You should do the same. I'll do the next visitation with Boyd. It's okay."

He welcomed the thought of allowing his brain to shut down for a while. With the extra pillows and a blanket in the closet, he made himself as comfortable as possible in one of those chair/beds which the hospital provided. They were comfy enough to spend a day or so, but not enough to make you want to stay for any length of time. It was abundantly clear hospitals weren't meant to be long-term facilities. That's what nursing homes were for.

Nursing homes. Jackson shook the thought from his head. He'd never get any rest if he allowed himself to dwell on the idea of Ma in one of those places.

The next thing he knew, he was spreading a blanket under the mimosa tree for him and Natalie. It was too hot out in the sun, but the tree, covered in little pink puffs, provided just the right amount of shade for them both. The light breeze moved a lacy pattern of shadow in a playful dance across her face.

She lay down on the soft blanket and he nestled in beside her, like two puzzle pieces clicking together. She let out a giggle as he touched her hair, her face, the outline of her breast. Then she pulled him to her, lips full and ready for his kiss, her body arching in response to it. He felt powerful in her presence; secure in his ability to please her; secure in her love for him. Although his soul never seemed as calm as it was when holding her, the desire in her eyes roused a beast he held within. Until now he had taken pleasure in ruling over the beast's ferocity, even as she guided his hand to the button of her jeans. She was ready for him to relinquish that power. Was he?

Opening his eyes, he blushed when he realized he was still in his mother's hospital room. No time to savor the sweet memory of the girl he once loved once and what seemed like forever ago.

"Hey there, sleepy head. Pleasant dreams?" Natalie asked.

Jackson rubbed his face in response, trying to wipe away any tell-tale sign of desire. "Anything but," he mumbled. "She still asleep?"

Natalie nodded.

"Did you visit Boyd already?"

She nodded again. "Been there and back. It was the last visitation of the day. Sorry."

He looked at the clock.

"Damn, it's so late. You should go home and get some rest."

"How will you get home?" she asked.

It seemed like days since he'd arrived by ambulance with Ma. And weeks since Boyd's accident. Time was out of whack. All that had taken place couldn't possibly have happened in the last two days. His brain felt muddy and thick.

"I'm going to stay here for the night. I'll worry about getting home tomorrow."

"Well, I'll be back in the morning anyway. I can always drive you out to your truck when you're ready."

He gave a stingy nod, not wanting to give the impression that he was eager to take any other help from her. Then he offered to walk her out to her car. It was late and the least he could do after all she'd done for Ma and Boyd.

As they walked, he reiterated, "I hope you know I appreciate everything you're doing for my family, Nat, I do. But you really don't need to be doing anything for me."

"Nonsense," she answered and then grinned. "Even frenemies deserve help when they need it."

He stepped back and raised his hands, admitting guilt.

"Hey, I don't blame you. I've been such a jerk to you and I can't even be sure why anymore."

"Oh, I know why," she answered.

He waited for her wisdom.

She looked at him as if she expected another response.

"Truth?"

He shrugged. "Truth it is."

As they stepped out into the night air she took a deep breath.

"Okay, here's my take on it, agree with it or not. I think the reason you've been such a jerk is because in all this time your feelings for me have never changed and that scares you. So you push me away because you're afraid to admit your father was wrong about anything. Somehow you think your world will come crashing down if it turns out he wasn't justified in taking his life. But he *was* wrong, Jackson, at least about us."

Jackson thought he saw her tear up, but she turned away. When she turned back, it was with resolve.

"I never would have held you back, the way your father said I would. In fact, I would have been happy to go with you on any adventure you wanted. We could have explored the world together. Or not. Whatever. I could have made you happy in any life you chose. I think deep down you know this and now you don't know how to go about admitting it to yourself or him or his memory. That's what I think."

Natalie struggled to find her keys in the dark as they arrived at her car.

"He wasn't wrong," Jackson insisted.

"Whatever," she returned in annoyance. "Think what you want. Do what you want. I don't care anymore. Someday you'll realize what you gave up just to protect him in nobody's mind but your own. You win. He was a saint. He killed himself because everyone else held him back and turned him into an alcoholic. It was everyone's fault but his."

He felt his face flush with anger. "You don't know what you're talking about."

She unlocked the door and opened it. "You're right. I don't. I don't know what it's like to lose a parent, especially to suicide and I don't know how it would affect me if I did. But I do know this. You were once your own person with your own dreams and now you think you have to give up yours to fulfill his. If your intention was to become your father, you're certainly headed in the right direction."

Then she got in and closed the door.

The engine turned over while he tried to come back with a response, something insightful and true which would shatter her false accusations. Because that's what they were – false. How could she say he wasn't his own person? The choice to leave had always been his. He wasn't trying to be Trevor Hawking. In fact, he was terrified of becoming just like his father, especially in death.

He shook his head, unable to allow her to be right.

"I'm not trying to be him!" he yelled as she drove away, peeling out of the parking lot. "I'm not anything like my father," he said to no one.

After standing in the quiet for a bit, his mind a mosh pit of whatevers and what ifs, he walked back toward the hospital entrance. Natalie suddenly drove up beside him and rolled down the window. He waited for some other condemnation from her.

"I'm sorry," she said in a calm voice. "I had no right to attack you in the middle of all this insanity. It was selfish of me and I apologize. You're nothing like your father, Jackson, you never were. Honestly, I always saw you as the stronger person." She glanced up at him, then back toward the steering wheel. "I'll be back in the morning. I hope by then you'll have some good news from the doctors. Good night."

"Good night," he answered as she drove away. *Stronger how?* If only he didn't wish she'd stay.

THE DEEPENING PIT

24

He was surprised to find his mother awake when he returned.

"How are you feeling, Ma?" he asked, touching her hand.

"Been better," she answered, still mumbling her words. "Afraid I'm going to be stuck like this."

The thought of her spending the rest of her life as an invalid tore at his heart. "No, Ma, I'm not going to let that happen, you hear me? There's gotta be ways to help get you back to where you were, at least. Some kind of therapy, or exercises, or something. We'll figure it out."

He let her know he was staying the night and she smiled. Then he asked her if there was anything she needed.

"Forgiveness," she said.

He raised an eyebrow. "Forgiveness? For what? You haven't done anything wrong, Ma."

He sat on the bed and brushed the hair back from her face.

"Been thinking," she said, slowly forming her words. "About your pictures. About your dad. I should have let him be the one to take those pictures and have those memories. I was selfish."

"What do you mean, Ma?"

She sighed. "I knew what he wanted to do with his life. I was afraid to let him go."

Of course. Dad had laid it all out, using Natalie as the example. Ma had been the rock tied to *his* neck, holding him down, drowning him in an unfulfilled life. Papaw might have been the one who talked about responsibilities and dedication to the family legacy, but Ma was the one who put on the restraints. He could have defied Papaw's wishes, regarded them as old fashioned, but without Ma's consent, he would never have left the mill to go off on adventures. He would never have abandoned his wife and children so selfishly. Even though that's exactly what he ended up doing anyway.

"You hate me?"

"For what?" he asked. "Being human? For wanting your husband home and fully vested in his family? Especially once Boyd was a part of it? Dad would have been gone weeks at a time in order to explore the caves he wanted to. And it's a dangerous business even now, Ma, just think how dangerous it would have been back then." Jackson thought of all the other men and women he caved with. Very few of them had significant others unless they were also part of the team. Not only that; caving was an expensive hobby. How would he have afforded it?

His mother had always been an active woman, but much more comfortable on the back of a horse than in the confines of rock. Caving was obviously not something they had in common or would do together. What woman would want to be left alone with two young, rambunctious and needy sons while her husband was off adventuring? After making the decision to take a wife and raise a family, his father should have been a happy man. What changed? Why wasn't he? Why weren't they enough?

Ma had nothing to be sorry for, his dad did. He'd known what she expected from him as a husband, and even if he didn't, he should have. He was the selfish one, not her. And if it was adventure he wanted, he could have found other ways to include her and his sons. The world was a vast and endless offering of possibilities. If he hadn't been so stubborn, he could have found a way to be happy.

Jackson touched her shoulder, hoping she could feel the warmth of his hand, and if she didn't, he hoped she felt the love he intended through it.

"I love you, Ma. There's no way in hell I could ever hate you for anything."

She smiled up at him, her eyes grey and misty. "I think about him every day, you know. I remember all the things I loved about him, all the beautiful moments I got to share with him, and there were many. He had this sweet romantic side that nobody ever saw but me. And he could make me laugh. I miss the man he was, but not the man he became. Is that wrong? Will I be judged for feeling that way? I can't help it. When I think of those times, it just makes me sad, or angry, so I try not to think of those things, but they have a way of seeping in." It was a lot for her to say, but she muttered her way through it.

Jackson thought about all the times he'd been angry since his father's death. Too often to count. He understood the guilt his mother expressed over feeling that way all too well and thought to commiserate with her about it, to let her know she wasn't the only one who got angry, but by the time he finished his train of thought, she was asleep. She must have worn herself out talking so much.

* * *

Early the next morning, the nurses came in, monitoring Ma's pain and preparing her for more tests.

Jackson waited impatiently for visitation hours to begin again in the ICU so he could go up to check on Boyd.

Nothing there had changed since the night before. Boyd was still in the same position with the same attachments dangling from his body. One of the monitors began beeping. Jackson jumped, thinking he should do something. He turned to go out to the nurse's station, but someone was already on it and heading his way.

"It's just the meds running out. I have to replace the bag," the nurse explained to him.

He wondered if the nurses ever got tired of having to explain again and again the most tedious parts of their job to the ignorant folk. For the nurses, a beeping machine meant nothing more than it would to a cook whose fries were ready to pull out of the oil. To an older brother worrying over his younger brother, it was an alarm which could be signaling the imminent death of his loved one.

The nurse set about her work, unplugging one set of tubes and inserting the new ones attached to a bag she suspended from a metal hook. Then she typed something into the computer.

As she typed away, Jackson asked her if there had been any improvement.

She looked at the screen.

"The doctor will be in soon for rounds. If you're here then, you can talk to her."

"I'll make sure I am," he said.

He spent the time he had talking to Boyd, hoping his words were getting through, telling him how much everyone missed him and how they were thinking about and praying for him, especially Ma. He apologized for their mother's absence, saying she was still recovering from everything that had happened.

"You need to come back to us, Boyd. We miss you so much. I even promise to take you caving when you're ready. There's a place just a couple hours away where we can drive right through the cavern and don't even have to get out of the car. Wouldn't that be cool? I'd do anything for you, Buddy. Anything to have you back home."

When he looked at Boyd, lying there so still, he saw him not as a boy anymore, but a man. Somehow he seemed different, and Jackson began to picture him as an old man, bent and slow-moving, his curls a mix of black and grey. Would he even be given the chance to grow old? Would he go on to adore Lindsey with as much enthusiasm as he did now? Jackson prayed his brother would be given the chance; that God wouldn't allow his light to burn out so quickly. Boyd deserved as much.

"I know I can't tell you what to do, Lord. I've ignored you lately, so why should you even listen? Except this isn't about me. It's not about what I want or deserve, it's about this guy right here. He's never hurt anyone, and if he did, I know he didn't mean to. It's not in him to be mean. His life is hard enough with all his issues holding him back. Don't make it harder for him, and don't take my saying not to make it harder for him as the reason to let him die. I know how this stuff works. I ask for something and then I get my answer in a way I never intended. That's not what I'm saying." Frustrated by his inability to articulate anything meaningful, he said, "Oh, you know what, never mind. This is why I stay quiet. Everything I say comes out wrong anyway. You're probably ignoring me too. You're probably not even listening."

"He's always listening, you know." He heard a female voice from behind him.

Jackson turned to see a doctor coming toward him. "Huh?" he asked.

"Mr. Hawking, here," she nodded toward Boyd. "Even when in an induced coma, his auditory function is still working. He just may not remember anything you've said when he wakes up." Sticking out her hand, she said, "I'm Doctor Wyeth. You are?"

"Mr. Hawking, uh, I mean Boyd's brother, Jackson. Nice to meet you, Doctor."

"Well, let's see what we've got here," she went around him and began typing on the movable keyboard, then went over to Boyd and lifted an eyelid, moving her penlight upward in front of his eye. She lifted his blankets and inspected the bandages on his legs and the scratches on his arms. "I hear he took quite a fall."

"Yeah," Jackson filled her in. "He was pretending to be Tarzan."

"Ah, yes, well, there's a reason why fictional characters are fictional," Doctor Wyeth mused.

Jackson agreed.

"Is there any improvement?" he asked.

"Temp's still elevated. Blood pressure too, but not as high as last night. At least it's going in the direction we want. The good news is, he's not in any pain."

"And that's it for the good news?" It didn't seem like much.

Dr. Wyeth looked him over, as if sizing him up for how much honesty he could take. "Right now, it's better than bad news. Here's what we know: we know he had a compound fracture of the left femur and several fractures in the right the ankle, along with various open wounds and abrasions. We don't know if he lost consciousness at the sight of the fall, but we haven't seen any signs of head trauma, which is very good. On the other hand, we know he lost quite a bit of blood. Consequently, he had to be resuscitated more than once not only in flight, but also in surgery. I'll be honest with you, Mr. Hawking, he's been through a lot already, and infections can be scary. More often than not we win the battle, but sometimes we're dealing with something very stubborn. The positives are he's young and he's strong and he has someone who cares about him. So let's stay in the positive and hope for the best. Okay?"

The young and strong line must be something doctors were taught to say to families in distress. Jackson was already trying to be positive. What he needed was something more, something tangible telling him what to do and giving him reassurance. All this uncertainty was making him nauseous.

He wanted answers, and he wanted them now. Problem was, what he wanted and what he got were two different things.

* * *

The news from Dr. Bratton wasn't much better. There had still been no change since the steroid shot.

"What about the plasma thing you talked about?" Jackson asked him. "Are we going to try that?"

The neurologist nodded. "Yes, we are starting the plasmapheresis today, but, as I said earlier, it is not always effective."

Jackson noticed the disappointment on Ma's face. He squeezed her hand and felt a faint return.

"Well, could you at least try to give her some hope?" he asked.

Without looking up from his chart, the doctor said, "Hmm. Well, of course there's hope. Why else would we be putting her through this therapy? Plasmapheresis is very much like dialysis, and although it isn't particularly painful, there is some discomfort, and it is a lengthy process."

That was hopeful? Considering the source, Jackson guessed it was the best they were going to get.

"The nurses will be in to get you prepped, Mrs. Hawking. We want you fully hydrated to reduce the possibility of side effects. The process takes several hours and will most likely be repeated another time or two, perhaps while you're in the rehabilitation center.

You'll be sent there for help with exercises and therapies which also may facilitate improvement in mobility. While in rehab, it will also be necessary to make plans for your living arrangements beyond rehab." He turned to Jackson. "Have you considered what we talked about yesterday?"

"What? Nursing homes? Not an option. We'll be taking her home."

The doctor nodded. "Very well. I'll have one of the nurses bring you some reading material on what services are available and what modifications she'll be needing."

Natalie came in as Dr. Bratton was leaving. Jackson stepped out into the hallway to call the insurance company.

The woman helping him was very nice, offering sympathy for his situation. After listening to her rattle off deductibles and copays, Jackson came away panicked about the financial catastrophe looming. He attempted to walk it off, avoiding the ICU, knowing it would only push him further into depression. When would there ever be any good news?

He stepped back into Ma's room and looked at Natalie.

"Can I take you up on that ride home? I need to grab some stuff from the house and get my truck."

"Sure," she answered and gave Ma a kiss goodbye.

Jackson leaned in and did the same, but lingered at his mother's forehead a little longer than usual. The responsibility to do the right thing for his family lay heavy upon him. He never felt so alone.

The drive home was a quiet one. Jackson noticed Natalie looking over at him, trying to figure him out, probably wanting to comfort him in some way, but he was so firmly planted in his own head he didn't have time for explanation or convincing.

He hated this world, but didn't want to leave it. He was bitter toward the mill but didn't want to sell it. He resented Natalie but didn't want to lose her. He was angry with God, but longed for His voice. He was overwhelmed by life, but didn't want to end it.

The world offered nothing but heartache. The same went for the mill, Natalie, God and life itself. What was the point of putting your heart and soul into something which gave nothing back? The mill would have to be sold, and the house, and the land. Jackson would need the money to pay for Ma's care, possibly Boyd's. Life would be a steady stream of doctors and wheelchairs and suicidal thoughts.

Maybe he should walk in his father's footsteps after all, right off the bridge.

PUNCTURE WOUNDS

25

Natalie dropped him off, but held onto his arm for a moment before he got out of the car, asking if he was alright. He told her not to worry, that he was tired and a bit overwhelmed, but that he would see her later. As soon as her car was out of sight he headed toward the cemetery.

Once inside the cemetery wall he greeted his grandparents by pulling a few blooming wild roses and placing them on their headstones. Then he sat between them.

"Hey, Nana. Hey Pap. I'm sorry to say, I have no good news. Ma's in the hospital, hardly able to move. She's scared she's going to be stuck as an invalid. Honestly, so am I. It's not fair. She's been through enough already, you know. You loved her like a daughter, so if there's anything you can do from your end to help her, it would be much appreciated." He sighed. "And then there's Boyd. What can I say? He's lying in the ICU," his voice broke as his throat closed, the familiar painful lump making its way to his nose. He shook his head to stop it, but the more he spoke about Boyd the more the gates of sorrow opened. "He doesn't deserve to lose his leg. He should be fishing and running and yuckin' it up the way he does. Neither one of them deserve this. Please help them if you can. Please... I don't know what else to do..." He was weeping now.

He sat with his head in his hands and allowed the pain to flow. "Please help us," he begged, as much to God as it was to his grandparents; anyone who was listening and able to assist. There had to be someone who could help or intercede on his behalf.

"Papaw's voice filled his head with a, "What's that yowling about, boy?" Something he used to say, especially to Boyd when he would cry out of frustration.

He wiped the tears from his face and regained some semblance of self-control, then stood up and stepped back on to his father's grave. He hadn't meant to, but there he was.

"Did you hear all that about Ma and Boyd?" he asked Trevor's headstone. "Do you care? Maybe if you're not too busy you could look in on them. They are your family, after all. Not that you give a shit."

Jackson reached over and grabbed a nearby wild raspberry cane, ignoring the thorns pushing into his skin.

"Here. This is for you. A good representation of your love for us." He placed the thorny cane atop the grey marble, then looked around. "No, wait, there's more," he said as he pulled another cane from the ground, this time noticing the small slits in his hands beginning to bleed. "Huh. Like every cut you made in me that night. What were your words? I was a disappointment to you?"

Jackson repeated the words which flowed so easily from his father, the man who managed to tower over him and make him feel small.

He gave in to the memory, allowed it to fill his vision, welcoming every punch in the gut and slash to his self-confidence. All the words his father spoke of - disdain for his legacy, his own father, Natalie. Jackson allowed the memory to come forward, the same way he allowed the tears to gush just minutes ago.

Listening to each insult his father lobbed at him and his responses to them, his own pathetic defense of Natalie and the love he felt for her roused his anger. Each claim his father made to warrant his unhappiness and convince Jackson he was destined to the same only intensified the rage building within him. He was once again standing on the bridge, the river below churning as furiously as the two men on it.

Trevor noticed his son's balled up fists and taunted him, pushing him to make the first move toward an all-out brawl.

Jackson swung for his father's jaw, but he was no match for Trevor, even in his drunken state. He grabbed Jackson's fist in his left hand. With his right, he slapped Jackson's face.

Jackson took a step back, freeing his hand.

"I had such hope for you," his father said. "You being a smart boy and all. I thought for sure you would take yourself out of here when you graduated, make something of yourself in the world. Didn't you appreciate all the things I tried to show you? See there was more to life than working that mill? No, instead you ignored what I taught you and listened to your Papaw and that girl."

"You have no right to even talk about Natalie," Jackson seethed, the sting on his face spreading to his heart. "She's done more for me than you ever have."

His father shook his head and laughed. "Go ahead. Be the pig content in his own shit." He sloshed sideward and then righted himself. "What a disappointment you are. Coward. You disgust me. I might as well jump from this bridge. Even Boyd has more ambition for life than you do." This time he lurched forward in his drunkenness, then took a moment to straighten himself up. "Go," he tilted his head. "Get the hell out of here and let me end my misery in peace." Then he held his hands out, asking, "Unless you'd rather watch?"

"Fuck you!" Jackson roared. "Go ahead and jump!"

He expected his father to hit him again. Instead, the man smiled.

A familiar rage burned through Jackson's body, setting off a furious burst of energy. He looked at his father's headstone and then wrenched thorny canes from their roots, sending clumps of dirt into the air. Blood flowed from punctures and scratches along his arms and the palms of his hands. He begged his father for relief.

"Even after the hell you put me through, I did what you wanted! I gave up everything I ever wanted to live out your dream! Not mine, yours! And where were you then? In all that time I looked for you, you were nowhere to be found! Not one whisper from you to say you were with me. Not one dream of you telling me I was on the right track! No vision of truth, no sign of approval! I looked and waited and not once would you give me any satisfaction. What more do you want from me? I tried to make it up to you!" Running out of steam, he pulled one last cane and held it out to his father's chiseled name. "You died for nothing!"

Then he threw the last wild raspberry cane down with the others.

The pain from his wounds was nothing compared to the despair he felt deep within his core. Nothing could divert his attention from it. Not even the small puncture wounds in his forearm put there by the fangs of a copperhead protecting its nest.

Jackson never noticed the snake as it slithered away through a hole in the rock wall.

He assumed the sudden lightheadedness came from all the exertion of the last few moments. Then he stumbled and fell into his father's headstone, landing among the discarded raspberry canes.

Blackness formed at the corners of his vision, pulling him under. He was powerless to stop it.

He had no idea how long it was before he heard a voice calling his name.

"Jackson." He opened his eyes.

He felt detached from his body, as if he were a few inches behind it, but still with it just the same. He looked out at his body, laying among the raspberry canes. Blood mottled his arms. At the end of his outstretched hands, a woman leaned toward him.

She had a round face and bright, smiling green eyes. She was wearing a long, calico blue dress. She reached out for him.

"Here, Jackson, let me help you up," she said.

She pulled to help him stand. He was a bit wobbly at first.

"How do you know my name?" he asked when he regained balance.

"Oh, I've known you all your life, my boy! I'm your great-great-great-great..." She began counting on her fingers. "Great-great grandmother. I think. Yes, six times. Let's see, there's Charlene, then Lettie, then Mary, then Silvie, then Katy, then me. Six." She finished counting again and then stuck out her hand to shake. "Lizzie Hawking. Elizabeth if you prefer to be formal, but my husband Edward never liked formality, so Lizzie will do."

FAMILY REUNION

26

Jackson took her hand and shook it slowly. "Am I dead?" he asked.

She smiled again. "No, not dead. Somewhere between the undiscovered country and a dream would be a better way to describe it. Snake venom can have incredibly different effects on different people. Some die, though, but not you, you being such a strapping, strong young man. Quite exciting, I think. Don't you agree?"

Jackson held his head. "I'm confused," he said groggily.

"Yes well, that is to be expected."

He looked around and everything else seemed as it should, the cemetery, the meadow, the house beyond it. Except there was an awkwardly cheery woman talking to him, claiming to be his long dead ancestor.

"Why are you here?"

"Me? I'm here to help you, my dear. You called out and asked for help, did you not?"

"Well, yes, I guess I did." Jackson scratched his head. "But help me do what, exactly?"

"Why, fall in love again, silly!" She clapped her hands excitedly.

Jackson was taken aback. "With Natalie?" he asked.

"No, not Natalie," she chuckled. "Everyone knows you're just as smitten with her today as you were the day you met."

"Everyone?"

"Yes," Lizzie motioned to all the headstones. "All of us. Your family. We all know how you truly feel about her, it's so obvious. And she's such a lovely girl. Once you wake up to the truth, you'll know it too." She patted his shoulder, reassuringly, then pushed on it playfully. "No, dear boy, we want you to fall back in love with your heritage! Remember how proud you once were to be a Hawking? Do you recall why you loved this place so much? How you and Boyd spent hours pretending to be pioneers building the early settlement?" Again she pushed on his shoulder, laughing. "You imagined yourselves to be Edward and me!" An idea she apparently found quite amusing. Taking his hand, she pulled him along the way Boyd used to when he was excited about some discovery. "Come. I have so much to show you!"

As unsteady as he felt, he allowed this pushy woman to direct him. They walked out of the cemetery and suddenly everything was different. There was no dirt road to walk along, or even the main gravel road which should lead to the house and the bridge beyond it. There was no house where it should be standing. When they got to the bluff, he realized there was no bridge, either.

"How?" he hesitated, looking for a way across.

"Here, take care, the path is steep." She led him down a narrow ledge to the dam crossing the river.

He found it much harder than he should have, his foot catching on rocks and roots. What was wrong with him, anyways? This should have been an easy descent. He'd hiked far more treacherous pathways in far more dangerous territory. Thank goodness for the woman holding on to his hand. If it weren't for her, he'd have made a total fool of himself by tumbling into the river.

At the bottom of the bluff was a dam crossing the river, slowing the flow of water for the mill wheel, but not stopping it.

"The rocks are quite slippery. You should be barefooted," she said as she unbuckled her boots. "If you fall, let the river take you to the spot where you fish with Boyd. You can walk back from there."

She traversed the dam like an expert, using a combination of raised skirts, arms and boots to keep herself balanced. The water surging over the dam was shallow, but powerful enough to knock anyone off their feet if they weren't careful. She seemed to take pleasure in the danger of it, turning back and laughing at Jackson's hesitation.

"Lucky it hasn't rained," she teased. "Or you would really find yourself in a pickle."

Making it across, she did a little hop, then climbed up the other side without replacing her boots or socks.

"Mother would be horrified, but I prefer bare feet to rigid leather boots. Especially before breaking them in. You can always tell when someone gets a new pair – they squeak like mice in a barrel!" She snorted and then laughed a hardy laugh to herself, throwing her head back and holding her stomach.

Then she waited patiently as Jackson slowly traversed the dam, giggling with every wobble along the way. When he reached her, she helped him to the ground.

She was a strange woman, but amusing. Middle-aged in appearance, but much younger in her demeanor. He imagined she would have been fun to know in her time.

"Here we go," she took his hand again and led him across the field to a low ridge, showing him the first house that she and Edward built together, with hand-hewn logs and mud from the river. "This is where we lived for the first year."

The house was small and rough, obviously built by hands new to the task. Jackson recognized the foundation rocks which still formed a corner wall in his own time. He and Boyd had used it as their fort many times, especially in winter during snowball fights. Was he really walking through the past with Elizabeth Hawking? How was this possible?

"Edward's brother William joined us then, along with his family and the parts to build a saw mill. I will tell you this... that saw mill made life much easier for us! With it we were able to build the grain mill and a new home just there." Elizabeth pointed to an area beneath a grove of Walnut trees where a cabin sat beneath their shade.

Jackson was sure nothing had been there a second ago. His eye went to the river where there now stood three buildings alongside it. Another cabin, a mill which was much smaller than the one he worked in now and next to that, a barn stacked with wood. Teeth from the giant saw peeked from behind the open barn door.

"People came from all over to buy our cornmeal and flour. Some brought wagons filled with fresh cut trees to be milled by that great, deafening saw." She covered her ears as if she could hear it still. Then she went on. "Will and his lovely wife lived in the cabin just south of the mill. What a pleasure it was to have another woman on the property! But then, such a shame. In the spring of 1849 they were washed away with the cabin and three of their children. Eddy and I raised up the surviving four children as our own, much like your mother and daddy did with Boyd."

"Did the mill get washed away then, too?"

"The grist mill flooded, but stood strong. The saw mill, as fortune would have it, did not."

"Papaw told me the whole thing was carried away in some big flood back then."

"That would have been during the Great Flood of '83, and after our son Henry had once rebuilt it." She pushed on his shoulder. "He was forced to rebuild, you know, after the soldiers took it upon themselves to destroy everything as that dang war was ending. You know that war between the states?" she asked as if he might not know.

"We call it the Civil War," he answered.

Lizzie clucked her tongue in annoyance. "Well, let me tell you, it was not civil at all. Those awful Jayhawkers ravaged these parts, killing and ruining good people, pretending they cared about politics to shoot entire families and take what they wanted. It never did matter what side you stood on during the war if you had what they wanted. We did our best to stay out of the whole mess and they murdered my dear Edward anyway. Shot him right through the door as he reached for his rifle. Evil people they were."

Papaw had explained to Jackson how most families kept their muskets readily available by hanging them above the front door of their cabins. It was a practice the Jayhawkers used to their advantage. Many a good man died trying to retrieve what he thought was his family's protection.

"Henry and his sons managed to survive that awful night, thank the Lord." She shook her head. "Those were horrible times for everyone, just horrible."

Lizzie waved her hand and Jackson watched it all play out in the landscape before him. A band of men shooting Edward through the door of his own cabin. Then, as the marauders moved on to Henry's cabin and attempted to kick his door in, Henry and his young sons snuck around through the trees and shot them all dead.

Then the scene changed. There was Henry, being held back as Confederate soldiers set fire to the mill, leaving him with no way to earn a living for his family.

"But our Henry never gave up," Lizzie said with tears in her eyes. "He and Silvie and their four boys did the best they could with what little they had."

As Lizzie told their story, Jackson watched in wonder as his ancestors rebuilt the mill in sped-up time.

"All the other mills fell to the turmoil caused by the war, but our Henry was determined to keep the family business going for his sons. Hawking's Mill was the only grain mill still in operation in this part of the country."

Suddenly, a great rush of water overran the land, the mill, the homestead. It even lapped at Jackson's feet.

"After surviving the Jayhawkers and that "less than civil" war, my son Henry drowned in the flood of '83, the one your Papaw told you about. Trapped in the wheel room there, Henry never saw what was coming." Lizzie shook her head in sorrow. "Lucky his wife Silvie was a well-respected woman in these parts. She'd been a good choice for our son. Had a golden tongue, she did, could talk you out of your boots. Did you know, she went to each and every one of the families in the area to ask their help in rebuilding the mill? A woman. A widow. She had to make them see it was just as much a benefit to them as it was for the Hawking family to keep the mill running. After all of the mills in these parts had been burned or raided, there was nowhere else to go. They were smart. Put their trust in that woman and pulled together to help her rebuild. They also built those two little cabins still standing there near the mill. One was used as the post office and the other housed a still."

"Boyd and I spent a lot of time playing soldiers in those cabins."

Lizzie smiled. "Yes, I watched you play, and before you, your father and uncle. And your Papaw before them. You see, Jackson, this land has held onto the hopes and wishes and love and laughter of every Hawking child Edward and I brought into this world, and on down the line. Some went off to search the world for happiness, which was their right, but the true Hawking men, men like my Edward, they stayed and made this place their dream. It can be a difficult life, yes, but a rewarding one, don't you agree?" She watched his face, waiting for an answer. "You did once. I saw you. You stood on that bluff overlooking your legacy and proudly shouted to the world, 'This all belongs to me!'" She even took "the stance", the same Peter Pan pose Jackson did, exuding all the confidence in the world he felt in that one moment.

A forgotten memory, but Jackson had no doubt it was real. Many times he stood on the bluff and surveyed the house and the mill and the residue left behind by men and women with the same blood as his coursing through their veins. It had been an invigorating notion, being part of something so tangible. He'd felt it every day; got caught up in the stories of strength and resilience. He'd never seen his ancestors as foolish in their drive to keep pushing forward, as his father did. At least not until that night.

"How many times has this place been torn down by some disaster, natural or otherwise?" he asked too quickly in what sounded like his father's voice, wiping sweat from his forehead. *When did it get so hot?*

She sighed and then smiled. "You already know the answer to that question, Jackson. Our history is like a cherished book burned into your memory. What you really want to know, or should I say, need to know, is this; has all the heartache and suffering been worth it? Isn't that right?"

Right as rain, he thought. Was it worth the sweat and blood? Was it worth the sacrifices he knew there would be? Was it worth his father taking his own life?

Lizzie stepped aside and there before him stood a man with a short beard, loose-fitting shirt and tattered wool pants held up by suspenders. He was old and worn, but smiled just the same. Jackson instinctively knew him as the second Henry, Papaw's father, who restored the mill after a fire in 1914. The same mill which still stood before him now. Henry also built the first bridge and the house on the bluff Jackson grew up in.

"Yer dern right it was worth it," Henry said in his cheerful hillbilly voice, "and I'd do it all agin if'n I had to."

Before Jackson could respond, another face appeared, that of Edward, Lizzie's husband and the original owner of the Hawking property. His was a kind and gentle face, but with a determined eye he caught Jackson's attention. This was a man with a vision and the courage to see it through.

"Walk with me boy," he said.

Jackson obeyed, following Edward toward the river.

"Some men look at a plot of land and see only dirt, perhaps a few clumps of grass for the snakes to hide under. It means nothing to them, inspires nothing within their being. Those men may find contentment in smoky rooms filled with money talk and political discourse and that's fine by me. But I tell you son, when my eye first fell upon this place, I felt a peace within my very soul. It was so much more than raw wilderness. Here were trees waiting to be carved into buildings and meadows offering feed for the livestock." He stepped up onto the bridge and leaned over the railing. "And a river daring me to harness it." Seeming satisfied with himself, he sat up on the railing. "I saw a farm, a mill, a distillery, a church, even a post office. A place to raise children, a sanctuary for the forgotten, a sweet spot for lovers and a resting place for the dead. Our little corner of the Ozarks has been and still is every one of those things. Don't you see it, son?" Edward jumped from the railing, stepped aside and extended an arm to expose the landscape from their vantage point on the bridge.

Jackson looked past Edward and saw a bustling place. Wagons full of grain lined up for unloading at the mill, the drivers sharing a quick swig from the whiskey barrel placed outside. Their faces shining with promise, women folk stepped out of the general store with baskets of flour and cornmeal and jellies, greeted by their neighbors. Boys huddled together by the river, eager to consider a friend's catch of the day or a young girl's smile. Jackson remembered seeing the mill alive like this, when he was younger and Papaw was still running things. Neighbors and church friends would come and have picnics under the oak trees, the same trees Henry and his sons hid behind to protect their home and surprise the Jayhawkers in the dark. They would fish in the same river which ebbed and flowed with the lives and deaths of their family. It was humbling to realize how much history took place on these few acres of land.

"No matter where you roam on God's green earth, you will never be as welcome as you are right here." The voice had changed. Papaw was standing before him, his eyes glistening with emotion.

"I tried my best to instill that notion in your father, but he never felt the same way I did about this place. I'm afraid I pushed him too hard and he resented me for it. I am sorry for that."

Jackson reached out to touch him. His hand tingled, but found nothing solid.

"Honestly, you could have been a bit kinder to him, Pap. But it was me who disappointed him in the end. I'm the one who's sorry. I even traveled the world trying to find him, to let him know how sorry I was for the things I said..."

"He knows," Lizzie's voice assured him.

The tingling began to make its way up his arm.

"But he never showed up. I never felt his presence, not in one damn cave. And I looked everywhere."

"Everywhere but here," Lizzie said, and she raised her eyes to the sky.

Not the sky. The roof of the mill.

Jackson followed her gaze and saw his father kneeling on the roof, a hammer in one hand, a piece of tar paper in the other.

"He's here?" Jackson's voice broke with dryness.

Trevor tapped at the tar paper and then turned toward his son. As their eyes met he smiled and then patted his chest.

Jackson pressed a palm to his own heart in acceptance of his father's silent message. This is what he'd been searching for all along.

"I can't believe he's here," he whispered.

"Yes, well," said Lizzie. "He never left. He's been working hard on himself, waiting for your return. Doesn't the mill look bright and shiny new?"

Jackson called out, "Dad! I've missed you so much!" He waved, but his arm felt weighted down, as if it were full of sand.

Trevor waved back, still smiling.

"Can't he talk?" Jackson asked.

He wanted to run to his father, in to the mill, up the steps and out on to the roof to join him, have the conversation they'd needed to have even if it took place straddling the roof line. He took a step and his legs turned to jelly. Dropping to the deck of the bridge, his focus stayed on his father.

"Why isn't he saying anything?" he asked again, without a care for his own predicament.

"Because Jackson, sometimes there are no words," he heard her answer.

She was right.

"Jackson? Jackson! Can you hear me?"

She was always right.

He was unable to see anything but a blur as he lost consciousness, but the voice was not Lizzie's. This voice belonged to Natalie.

EMERGENCY ROOM
ROMANCE

27

He opened his eyes and tried to focus and there she was, kneeling beside him, taking his hands in hers, examining them.

"Jackson?" Her voice was high pitched and panicked. "You're bleeding!" She looked him over. "What happened?" she asked. "Can you hear me? Please say something!"

He tried, but the words garbled in his mouth. It seemed everything was turning to jelly.

"Oh my God!" Her eye stopped at a point on his forearm. "I think you've been snake bit! It's so swollen!" She looked around, eyes wide and frantic.

"It's all right," Jackson told her. "I'm fine. My dad's here. Everyone is here. You're here. I'm so glad you're here. I've missed you so much, Natalie. I was so stupid to push you away. You were right about everything. I was stupid to run off and try to find my father in every place but where he's been the whole time. Right here with Ma and Boyd and you. With you. Where I should have been all this time. Can you forgive me?"

Natalie grabbed his chin and tried to force his mouth apart.

"I can't understand a word you're saying! Is your tongue swollen? Can you breathe?!"

Jackson pushed at her hands, but she held tight. "I'm fine," he said, "I'll show you."

His intention was to stand up to show her how fine he was, but he never got past pushing up on his elbows. He willed his legs to pull together, but they refused to cooperate. Nothing seemed to be working right, not his legs or his hands, not even his face when he smiled at her. That only seemed to frighten Natalie more.

He heard the word hospital and a lot of Jesus' while she attempted to lift him into the car.

Jackson's dead weight was no easy feat for her. Even with the muscles she sported from lifting and carrying heavy boxes and flour sacks, Jackson chuckled at the sight of her lifting his hulking 6'3 body off the ground.

"Glad you think this is so funny," she said.

Grunting, she lugged him up into the front seat.

He hoped she wasn't expecting him to drive. Then he heard the passenger door open and felt her pull him across the seat, letting out a long growl as she did, like a woman in labor pushing out a baby. He looked up at her, jaw set and determined, her face beaded with sweat, hair wet around the edges. *This is what she would look like delivering our babies.* His thoughts swirled with the idea of it, made his heart race. The next thing he knew, she was buckling him in.

For someone who chastised his reckless driving, she certainly gave herself permission to do the same. Trees and cars blurred by on the ride back to town, making Jackson nauseous. He leaned against the window with the AC thankfully blowing directly into his face.

"Slow down," he garbled.

She looked toward him, then back to the road.

Did she hear what I said? He flopped his hand atop hers and squeezed as best he could. Partly to slow her driving down, partly to let her know how much he loved her. At least he was pretty sure he was squeezing her hand. The tingling felt stronger there.

* * *

"He's lucky the bite was fairly shallow," said the ER doctor. "We'll clean up the wounds, pull out the thorns and give him a tetanus shot and an antibiotic. He can expect a few more hours of weakness in his extremities, but he should be fine after that."

"Seeing him collapse like that," Natalie's raspy voice broke, "I just panicked."

"Understandable," said the doctor. "You've had a good scare."

Jackson reached out to grab her hand, to offer some comfort, and missed his target.

"Oh, and his perception might be off for a while too," chuckled the doctor.

"Thanks for everything," Natalie said as he left the room.

Jackson tried again to reach her. This time Natalie caught his hand and held on tight. He pulled her closer to the bed and met her eye.

He wanted to try again to tell her all he was feeling, but he knew it would have to wait until he could say it clear enough for her to understand. Instead he leaned in and attempted to kiss her, again missing his target. She took control by cupping his face and kissed him on the lips.

"Is that what you were going for?" she asked and then kissed him again.

He had to tell her. She had to know how all the idiotic behavior toward her had been a cover for the feelings he had tried so hard to ignore. She had to know how right she'd been about his fears. She deserved to know how he really felt.

He gave a crooked smile, wishing he could control his mouth. He needed to tell her how he may have left her three years ago, but how she had never left him. In his mind. In his heart. He had never stopped thinking about her. He had never stopped loving her. It had always been her.

His instinct was to blurt it all out but all he could do was smile.

She returned the gesture. "I know," she said. "You can tell me all about it when your tongue starts working again."

He blinked. She was so smart.

"Well, good enough for talking, anyway," she said with a grin.

* * *

Gradually his abilities returned. When he was able to speak clearly enough and Natalie was back from checking in on Ma and Boyd, he asked her to sit close while he recounted his walk through history with Lizzie and his long dead family members.

She listened intently to every word without a word, smiling in the right places, frowning where he would expect, seeming to be as caught up in his excitement as he was. He began to wonder if she believed his fantastical account or was only appeasing him, chalking it up to a snake bite delusion, but then he realized it didn't matter. The experience would always be his to cherish no matter what conclusion she came to.

He got emotional when he described the exchange between himself and his dad.

"...and there he was, perched on top of that peak like he belonged there, even though I've heard him bitch about being up there to fix holes after hail storms I don't know how many times. He definitely never did it with a smile." Wistful tears filled his eyes.

"Well, the smile was for you, don't you think? And the hand over his heart. I'm sure he was trying to tell you how much he loved you."

Jackson nodded. "I think you're right. I just don't understand why he didn't say a word, not even a 'Hey'. Or why he was on the roof of the mill to begin with." He scratched his head. "I don't get it."

She shrugged. "My Grandmother sometimes comes to me in my dreams and never speaks a word. She takes me places or shows me things without ever making a sound."

"But this wasn't a dream." He couldn't help but be defensive.

"Oh, I know." She said it cheerfully, as if there were no doubt in her mind. "I just mean it's not unusual for messages from the other side to be unspoken." She paused, drawing in a thoughtful breath. "Just so you know, I don't doubt anything you just told me, Jackson. Whether it was snakebite driven or not doesn't make it any less real. It still happened. I truly believe your ancestors reached out to you today."

"Thanks." He nodded. "I can see why they love you so much."

"Your ancestors talked to you about me?" She chuckled.

"Yep. Lizzie made it very clear that I was the only one with any doubts about how I felt, and the sooner I figured it out the better."

"Oh really?" she teased, "There were doubts?"

He cringed at the thought of how badly he had treated her.

"What an asshole I was. I'm sorry. You didn't deserve any of that."

She didn't argue with him and he didn't expect her to.

"You were right that night in the parking lot. I was so afraid of allowing myself to feel what I was feeling, I did everything I could to push you away." He lifted her hand and kissed it. "And all I've really wanted to do since I got back is drown in those chocolatey eyes and follow that crackly voice wherever it leads."

"I have a crackly voice? Is that supposed to be a compliment?"

He nodded. "Yeah, crackly, raspy, sexy, whatever you want to call it. I missed your voice. I missed talking to you. I missed us." He pulled her hands close to his chest, meeting her eyes.

"I missed us too," she said in a quiet voice.

He had so much to make up for. He had betrayed her trust and broken her heart. What if their relationship was so damaged, it could never be the same?

"Do you remember that party at Jacob Forrester's house? The one where you stared at me like some crazy stalker chick all night?"

"I wasn't stalking you. I had a crush on you. That's what teenage girls do when they're crushing on someone."

"Well, you probably went home thinking I never even noticed you, but I did. You and your friends were a little too drunk for the walk home so I followed you to make sure you got there safe. Y'all were so loud and giggly you never even realized I was right behind you the whole time."

Natalie's head tilted in surprise. She grinned. "Now who's the stalker?" She nudged him.

"I remember standing outside your house, thinking, *a good family lives here*, you know, it's such a happy looking house."

She looked at him oddly.

"And then I saw you at the window. Talking to the moon like it held your secrets. I knew then that I wanted to be the one you told those secrets to."

She shook her in disbelief. "Who are you?" She asked.

"I'm the guy who's going to spend his life making sure he's worthy of you."

"You are worthy, Jackson. You always have been."

"Not lately I haven't. I love you so much, Natalie. I want you to know that I've never wanted to be with anyone but you, before I left, or since. Through all the stupidity and wandering, I've only ever loved you."

Her eyes seemed to sparkle. "I'm so glad you finally figured that out."

She leaned in and kissed him and for a moment, the world faded away. No vision of his father screaming in his face, no fear welling up in his gut, causing him to flee. When their lips parted, he heard the words he longed to hear, the words that expressed forgiveness as well as affection.

"I love you Jackson Hawking. Always have and always will."

He took a breath of liberation, if only for that instant. It felt so good. He wanted the freedom from guilt and trepidation to last, but that meant their conversation wasn't done. If he was going to feel truly liberated, there was more to be said and secrets to be revealed.

"I never should have let him talk me out of what I knew was the truth."

Those chocolate brown melty eyes smiled at him and he sighed.

"I let my dad's crazy become my crazy and I'm sorry. I never stopped to think how much it affected anyone else. How it affected you." He let go of her hands, giving her the freedom to be angry by what he had to say next. Or perhaps saving himself from the sign of rejection. What he had to say wasn't something he was proud of. "I need to be totally honest with you. Y'all think I've stayed away 'cause I was off on this grand exploration for the past three years, but the truth is, I stopped caving a while ago."

"Oh?" she asked, with another tilt of the head. "How long ago was that?"

See? That's where she would have let go.

"A year, maybe closer to a year and a half."

The last thing he wanted to do was cause her any more pain than he already had, but if he was going to dive in, he had to do it without holding back.

Here goes. "Well, I had this experience in Mexico, out in the middle of nowhere. I was getting ready to repel into the deepest sink hole I'd ever seen. My partner Dave and I, we were all harnessed up and just starting the descent. I decided to take some pictures before we got going." He looked over at his belongings on the chair. "Here, grab my phone for me, would you?"

She pulled his phone from the pocket of his pants and handed it to him. He then flipped through and showed her the same pictures Joy had seen of the deep sinkhole with hanging vines.

"Dave was holding on to me while I hung upside down to get these shots."

"Wow. That's deep!" Natalie seemed impressed.

It felt strange to be showing her these pictures now, after all this time. She should have been the first person to see them.

"Something weird happened to me while I was hanging upside down there, Nat. I don't know what brought it on, seems like it came out of nowhere. This...this thought popped into my head. Clear as if someone was talking in my ear. But it wasn't someone else's voice, it was mine. And this voice tells me to push the button on my harness and let myself go." His hands exploded out from his head. "I'm hundreds of feet in the air! What the fuck, right? Where did that come from? And then I watched myself drop over four hundred feet to the floor of the cave. I heard the thud, all my bones snapping when I hit. I could even smell the guano and the moss all mixed with my blood. As if it was actually happening. What the hell?" He rubbed his face as if to wake himself from a dream. "It was the most terrifying moment of my life."

Natalie stared at him, then cleared her throat. "Well, at least you had the presence of mind not to act on it."

"You want to know what was the scariest thing? As real as those pictures in my head were?" He wagged his finger. "Not nearly as terrifying as the fact that I had to talk myself out of doing it. As if I really would." He threw himself back onto the pillow. "Why? Why would I think those things?" He wasn't expecting an answer, but he would have loved one. "When Dave pulled me up, he saw how white my face was. He thought I'd passed out. I should have backed out of the climb right then, but I didn't want anyone to know, so I told him I was fine. That was a lie. The most irresponsible thing I've ever done, and there's a list, I know you know. I could have gotten people killed. As soon as we were back up top, I apologized to the team for putting them in danger and sold my gear to whoever wanted it. I'll never go back in a cave again."

"Never say never. I doubt it was the cave that brought that on." Natalie rubbed her chin. "Has anything like that happened since then? I mean, have you had other thoughts about hurting yourself?"

If he told her the truth, would she think he'd lost his mind? *Had* he lost his mind?

The truth. All of it if he wanted to be free.

He nodded. "All the time. I could be anywhere. In the middle of the day and boom, I'm suddenly running my truck into a tree, or slicing myself open with a knife or...or falling down an elevator shaft."

"Jackson!" She pulled back in horror. "Seriously?"

"It's messed up, I know. Scares the shit out of me, too. What the hell is wrong with me?" he asked, begging her for answers.

Shaking her head, she stumbled over her words. "That's - terrifying. I-I don't know. Maybe - maybe it's all the trauma you've been through. Like PTSD, or something. Or part of the grieving process. I'm not sure. But there has to be an explanation. You can't be the only one who has thoughts like that. I'm guessing you've never told anyone else about this."

He barely shook his head, embarrassed to admit any of it.

Taking his shoulder, she said, "Don't worry. I'll help you find out what's going on, okay?"

Nodding, he gave a weak response. "Okay," he said from far away.

"You have to promise me something." She took his face in her hands. "Are you listening?"

"Yes, I'm listening."

"You promise me," she said, softly jabbing his chest, "if you do ever have a thought like that again, you will tell me right away. I mean it. I can't help you if you keep secrets from me."

"I promise." He took the hand jabbing his chest and held it against his heart. "I promise I'll tell you everything, no matter how crazy it is. I don't want to die."

"You're not going to die, Jackson. We're not finished with you yet."

"We?" he asked. Did she intend to fill Ma in on the crazy?

"God and me," she said, "I'm pretty sure He has plans for you too."

"Oh, great," he said flatly.

"Good things," she replied. "Only good things from now on." She blew a long breath out. Then she raised an eyebrow. "You said you stopped caving over a year ago. If that's true, then where have you been all this time?"

Not where I should have been, that's for sure. So much time wasted. On what? Selfish insecurities? Grief he seemed incapable of handling on his own? Wandering aimlessly while his family needed him most?

While his mother and brother grieved for their husband and father. While Ma endured the symptoms and diagnosis of Multiple Sclerosis. Jackson imagined Boyd worrying over their mother, Natalie beside them, doing her best to keep them all strong. He was the one who should have been doing that.

He should have been home, mourning alongside the people he loved, the only people who could possible understand what it was like to lose someone to suicide.

How could he help Natalie understand the depths of his stupidity when he didn't understand it himself?

"After my freak out in the cave, I came back to the states and wandered around for a while. I didn't know what to do. I wanted to come home, but I didn't feel like I could. I was afraid I'd let Ma down. Again." He looked down at their now clasped hands, stroked her skin with his thumbs. "I was so at odds over you. As if this battle constantly raged between how much I missed you and how much I resented you. Coming back to you meant betraying him. I couldn't love you both." *And I resented the wrong person for it.* "I ended up in Memphis and took a job working on the docks. I was stuck. Like my feet were planted in the mud."

"Indecision can do that to you," she said, returning the affection.

"I guess," he said with a shrug. Then he looked up at her, ready to face the truth. "I didn't want to have to face you and admit I'd been wrong all along. I was ashamed of myself and pissed at you for making me feel that way. But it wasn't you who was making me feel that way. It was him." He sighed. "I should have trusted my first instincts and stayed with what I knew would make me happy. *Who* would make me happy," he corrected himself. "Do you think you can forgive me for breaking your heart just to appease a dead man?"

168

She squeezed his hands. "I never blamed you, Jackson. You were following your heart."

"See, that's the kind of stuff he would say was a bad thing. Your ability to understand someone else's stupidity and not hold it against them is something I've always loved about you. I let him twist it all up in my head and doubted everything I thought I wanted."

"I've always known what I wanted," she said, her voice happy and confident. "That's never changed. It's always been you, your family, even the spirits of the dead folk walking around. I can't think of anything that would make me happier than a life at the Hawking place. It's where I belong." She paused. "Tell you what. I'll forgive the crazy and even the prolonged absence. I know you never meant to break my heart. So let's put that behind us, okay? Right now we need to concentrate on getting everyone healthy again."

"I agree. If they don't get in here soon with the discharge papers, I'm going to leave without them. I need to get back upstairs."

"But you know," she teased, "even though I've forgiven you for being such a jackass, there are still a few things you might do to make up for the pain and suffering you put me through."

Jackson laughed. "Is that right?"

"Umm-hmm. A few foot rubs would be nice, maybe some romantic dinners, you know there have been a lot of new restaurants opened in the area since you've been gone."

"Anything for you, my queen," he said, bowing his head. "I am from this day forward your faithful and loving servant."

He kissed her hand.

"And don't you forget it." She smiled.

NOTHING GETS BY MA

28

Not wanting to frighten Ma, Jackson had asked Natalie to make excuses for his absence while he recovered in the ER. As much as he wanted to get to Ma, he almost wished he'd be released too late for visitation. Then he wouldn't have to explain the puncture wounds and the scrapes, or the crazy, weird half dream/half hallucination he shared with his ancestors. No such luck. Visitation ran til ten o'clock on her floor.

The first thing Ma said was, "Let me see your arms."

Lifting an eyebrow, he looked at Natalie. "Snitch," he said holding out bandaged arms to his mother.

"What were you thinking?" she mumbled.

Jackson shrugged. "The raspberries were trying to take over the cemetery. I guess I got carried away."

"Ya think?" she asked.

He wasn't ready to spill his guts to Ma just yet. With a downward look and a tilt of the head, Jackson asked Natalie to step in.

"Well, that's what happens when you let your anger get the best of you. You let down your guard and the copperhead sinks his teeth in," she said with a smirk.

Jackson returned with sarcasm. "Thanks for the help."

Ma's eyes shifted from Natalie to Jackson and back again.

"What's going on with you two?" she mumbled before turning to Jackson. "You finally come to your senses?"

He let out a laugh, then corrected himself with a cough. "Dang, Ma."

"'Bout time."

"How does she know these things?" he asked Natalie.

Natalie raised her palms in surrender. "I have no clue. She's your mother."

"Hallelujah," said Ma.

* * *

Ma's appointment for the plasma exchange was early the next morning. As uncomfortable as she must have been, she smiled throughout the treatment, catching glances between her son and the love he had worked so hard to sabotage. They were telling glances, finally free from Jackson's self-imposed restrictions. Free to let his love shine through. Free to begin again.

This time, as they prayed, he joined hands with them, although he let Ma and Natalie send the "signals" to the "brain". He had come to understand how powerful words could be and the two women he loved best seemed to know the right ones to say. He chose to keep his prayers silent; prayers of gratitude for what he witnessed the day before, either real or imagined. Prayers of gratitude for the choice it now allowed him and the peace he felt for making it. Even after the praying was done he held on to Natalie's hand, keeping it safe in his lap.

The results of the cleansing of Ma's system came on within a few hours. It began with a wiggle in her toes, then a strong grip from her fingers before the paraparesis began to release itself from her legs. As the tingling faded, recognizable sensations returned to her body.

The joyous trio became giddy with Ma's progress throughout the night and into the next day. It was important for her to enter rehab with the confidence she needed to exercise herself back to mobility. Yes, it would be hard physical work, but she felt up to the challenge.

It wasn't until the doctors confirmed she was on the road to recovery that Jackson told her about Boyd, his weakened condition and how they'd almost lost him again.

"I feel awful, you know, he hardly had any visitors in the past two days. By the time I came out of my copperhead trip, we'd missed the last visitation," he said with a sigh, wondering what awaited him in Boyd's room. The progress of the last 24 hours had swept him up in a stream of optimism. Thinking of Boyd and his dire situation brought his good mood to a halt. "I'm headed down to see him now. Natalie will stay here with you," Jackson explained to Ma.

"You're not going alone," Ma said. "I'm going with you."

Jackson was not surprised.

"I don't care if you have to wheel this whole damn bed down there. I'm going to see my son."

He knew this argument was unwinnable, so he asked for a wheelchair at the nurse's station. At first they balked at the idea, until Jackson explained to them that once his mother's mind was made up she would find a way, with or without their help.

As soon as they stepped into Boyd's room Jackson noticed a difference. It was much quieter without the machines whirring and hissing. Boyd was breathing on his own again.

The doctor came in with good news: the infection was finally under control and they were in the process of bringing him out of the coma.

Natalie wheeled Ma over to the bed and with her assistance, Ma reached out and touched Boyd's hand. His eyes opened and looked directly at Jackson.

Jackson smiled, misty-eyed. "Hey, Bud. Look who's here."

Boyd turned his head and looked at Natalie and then Ma, who removed her required mask so he could recognize her.

"Once again we welcome you back to the land of the living," Ma said before she broke into sobs.

Natalie squeezed her shoulders.

Boyd turned back toward Jackson with a blank expression.

"I know this isn't all making sense to you yet, Buddy, but it will. Just give it some time and know we're here and we love you. And when you're ready – man have I got a story to tell you!"

THE WIND WHIPS UP ANSWERS

29

One breezy Sunday afternoon Jackson asked Natalie to take a walk before dinner. He brought her up to the cemetery where he'd found himself spending a lot of time in the last few weeks since the "family reunion", talking to his ancestors and listening for answers.

Natalie asked about any progress he might be making in his therapy sessions.

"Sometimes it feels like progress and sometimes it doesn't, honestly. I'm not sure it's even helping, but my therapist says that those times I feel like I'm being tortured are a sign that it is working. Mostly I'm just learning how to deal with the things I used to panic about."

"I would say that's progress. I'm glad you found someone you could talk to."

"I'd say I already had that." Jackson purposely bumped into her, sending her off balance and then grabbing her arm to right her.

"Gee, thanks," she chuckled. "Is that how you show your appreciation?"

"Not usually," he said as he pulled her into his arms, kissing her lips and then around her face and neck, more and more playfully as he went, until she was giggling and pulling away. "That better?" He asked.

"That was okay," she said, "for a child. I want a proper thanks, now, if you don't mind. After all, I am your queen, remember?"

He bowed his head. "How could I forget?" He then took her hand and kissed it gently before taking her face in his hands and kissing her properly. "I am your eternally grateful servant."

The chocolatey eyes he loved so much smiled back at him. "Eternally. I like that," she said and then kissed him full with promise.

* * *

A warm southern wind pushed against them as they walked, slowing their steps.

"Watch for snakes," Natalie warned him as they stepped over the wall.

"At least they can't hide in the brush anymore," he said, showing off the scars he sustained from pulling at the wild raspberries. "I made sure there was nothing left."

"Something that might have been easier to do with gloves on." She gave a sly smile.

"Yep, I do remember having that same thought somewhere along the way." He led her along a patch of brown grass to the older side of the cemetery. "I'm not sure how they did it before the bridge was built, but someone had the sense to bury the dead up here and away from the floods. I'm not sure why it took them so long to build the homestead up here, too. Here, this is Richard's marker, or what's left of it. He was the first born of Edward and Elizabeth. He was also the first Hawking to die on this land. Some childhood disease, I think."

They stood before a flat, odd-shaped stone leaning precariously in the dirt. Its carved letters were barely visible.

"I can't read the dates," said Natalie, bending over the grave.

"There are quite a few of them like that - too weathered to read. I think he was about five or six when he died. Here's Edward," he pointed to another thin rock protruding from the ground. "And Lizzie next to him."

Putting his arm around Natalie's shoulder, he introduced her to the woman who made him fall in love again.

"Lizzie, this is Natalie, but of course you already know that. My one true love, same as Edward was to you. We promise we'll continue what you started and make this place something we can all be proud of."

"Wish I could have met you in person, Elizabeth," Natalie said to the gravestone. "I think we might have been great friends."

Jackson glanced over at Natalie, a spark of adoration in his smile. "I do believe you would have," he said slowly, allowing his eyes to rest on her.

It took a moment for her to notice his gaze before she blushed in response, but the moment was short-lived.

A sudden wind, coming from the north, chilled them both and drew their attention upward, toward the massive dark cloud bank pushing toward them from the west.

"Front's coming in fast," she observed.

"That's a wall cloud," he said, stepping back.

As they watched it approach, the wind shifted direction. Clouds swirled, lifted and lowered.

Natalie took out her phone, "I'll check the radar."

"I don't need the radar to show me, I can see it plain as day! It's definitely lowered and yep, and there's a freakin' funnel trying to form. See it? We need to move."

He took her hand and pulled her toward the cemetery wall, then helped her jump over it.

"The weatherman only said possible thunderstorms! They never said anything about severe weather!" she complained.

Both of their phones went off with the local news chime, signaling a weather alert.

"Well, they are now! Thanks for the warning!"

Off in the distance the tornado sirens wailed, one up by the highway, its warning blasts circling through the hills, while the second one down in the marina bounced its signal across the lake.

As they ran across the meadow, Jackson kept his eye on the swirling clouds above them. The approaching funnel descended and rose, as if trying to make up its mind whether or not to stretch out to the earth. The air became strange and the wind whipped against them, howling in their ears.

"Forget trying to make it back, it's here! Lay down in this ditch!" He pulled her down with him into what was barely a depression in the earth.

They watched in horror as the thirty foot wide funnel made its way to the ground only yards away, dragging its destructive skirt about a foot past the cemetery wall before picking itself up again. As it passed over them, the eerie pressurized whistling pierced their ears.

The funnel hovered for a moment just beyond them as if deciding which direction to take. Then the twisted rope descended again, headed for the dirt road leading to the house. The ground trembled beneath them as it set down.

"Ma!" Jackson yelled. He tried to get up, to go and save his family, but Natalie held on fast.

"No!" she cried. "You can't outrun it! Stay with me! Please!"

He knew she was right. The tornado had a head start. He couldn't outrun it, and if it did hit the house, debris would fly in all directions and possibly at him. He had no intention of dying today.

With a deafening thunder-train rumble, the tornado blasted dirt and grass outward and upward, filling its cone and the air around it. Jackson could hardly see its path through the dust. He waited breathlessly for the house to explode into splinters.

To his relief, it didn't. At the last moment the twister changed its course, turning at the road alongside the house, following the road to the bluff where it began to ascend, but not before it crossed the river and caught the very top of the mill. As the funnel blended back into the clouds, debris rained down on the oak trees where Henry and his sons once hid from the Bushwhackers.

Small hail began to pelt Jackson and Natalie. They ran for the house.

"Oh my God!" Ma screamed from the porch. "Are you all right? Are you hurt?"

They were doubled over, trying to catch their breath. Ma and Boyd were busy touching them and checking for injuries, but found nothing but disheveled hair and clothing.

As his breath came back to him, Jackson held on to Natalie's shoulders. They looked at each other and began to laugh.

"Do you believe that? Oh my God!"

Natalie shook her head, laughing.

"What's so funny?" asked Ma.

"Other than we were this close to a tornado?" Jackson pinched his trembling fingers together. "Did you see where it hit the mill?"

Natalie nodded her head, giggling, her eyes filled with tears.

Jackson took her in his arms and held her tight, laughing still.

"It hit the mill? That's not funny!"

"Come here. I want to show you all something."

He led his family to the edge of the bluff. Debris hung in the trees below and scattered across the ground around the mill.

"He knew. That's what's so funny."

"What do you mean? Who knew what?" asked Ma.

"Dad. The mill. I get it now. He knew what was going to happen."

"He knew about the tornado?" asked Boyd.

"Look there," Jackson pointed to the roof. "You see those missing tiles? They're the exact same tiles he was fixing when I saw him that day I told you about. He never said a word but I knew he was trying to tell me something. He was trying to tell me it was going to be okay. He was trying to tell me he's here to help."

"You think he likes it here now?" Boyd asked, his hands clasped together, eager for a yes.

Jackson held on to Natalie as hard as he could. His body shook from the adrenaline rushing through him.

She returned with a reassuring squeeze.

"I think he finally appreciates what a treasure this place is. He was so stubborn it took the most messed up thing he could do to learn that, but now he sees what makes us all stronger. He wanted me to know that this gift from Edward and Lizzie is well worth the blood and sweat and yes, tears, to keep it. This place is our family's legacy and it's worth fighting for."

"Damn right it is," said Ma, and all but one laughed.

Boyd only raised an eyebrow and held his hand out toward her, waiting for the quarter he'd add to his jar.

A MODEST PROPOSAL

30

Even after Ma spent six weeks in a rehab facility where exercise helped to rebuild the strength in her body, and then another plasma exchange improved her overall stamina, a residual weakness in her legs persisted. The doctors claimed she would need a walker to get around, but getting Ma on board with that was a slow process. She stubbornly resisted the idea of an "old-lady" walker at first, but as time went on, she increased her agility and therefore her speed with it, making her feel more comfortable and not so old. There were other dangerous falls to come and days she tired quickly. Some days she would need to take the afternoon off to rest, and wasn't so stubborn about doing it. It would be a few more years before a wheelchair became necessary and permanent.

Through it all, Jackson was there to cheer her on, encourage her imagination and help bring her visions for the mill to life.

One of Ma's dreams had been to create an artist's retreat, not just an "artist's corner" in the shop but something much more substantial and that's exactly what they accomplished. Jackson built a grouping of cabins near the mill to her specifications, up off the ground for protection from future flooding, where artisans could come to perfect their artistry. The craftsmen then displayed and sold their wares in a historically accurate early 1900's era "town" built just for them. Potters and silversmiths, furniture builders and leather workers all had their own shops. "Hawking's Mill Village" became a tourist attraction of its own and brought in enough money to take care of any needs Ma and Boyd might have in the future. All it took was Ma's vision and Jackson's desire to see it through to make it successful.

* * *

As for Boyd, a month-long hospital stay and then a two-month "sentence" in rehab (Boyd constantly complained he was being "tortured"), was celebrated with a homecoming party. Lindsey and Joy were invited for dinner, but before they arrived, Ma had a surprise for Boyd.

The family sat together on the porch, Ma's despised walker beside her, her favorite purple cane beside Boyd's chair now. From her pocket she pulled a small box.

"Here Boyd, this is for you." She handed him the box. "I asked Jackson to take it to the jeweler's to have it cleaned up and looked at."

Boyd opened the box and was excited to see the ring he'd found near the pond.

"Wow. It looks so pretty now," he said as he turned it over in his hand.

"Well," said Ma, "turns out, it is a real ruby. You were right."

"I was?" He seemed surprised.

She went on. "Yep, and it's real 14kt gold, too, so it's worth a lot of money."

"Wow!" he said again and showed it to Jackson and Natalie.

"The jeweler says the setting was popular back in the early 1800's, so it must have been one of your great-great-great grandmother's, or aunt's or some such person."

"From Civil War time?" he asked.

Ma nodded. "Maybe. Or even earlier than that."

"Wowy-wow wow," he repeated. "I better take good care of it, right?"

"Well, Bud, that's what Ma wanted to talk to you about. Remember how you wanted to give it to Lindsey?"

"To 'prose to her?"

"Yeah, to propose to her. Are you still wanting to do that?"

Without hesitation, he gave a hearty, "Heck, yeah!"

Ma giggled. "Well, there you go then. She'll be here soon. Why don't you go figure out what you want to say to the girl of your dreams?"

In his excitement, he jumped up from his chair and then quickly sat back down from the pain.

"I keep forgettin'," he said with a sigh.

Then he took the cane and tried again, more slowly, with a slight wince as he put his full weight on his feet. His recovery would take time the doctor's said, and it could be a year before he might not need the cane. Even then he would walk with a limp, an idea Boyd found pretty cool.

"I have a character now," he'd say.

"You are a character," Jackson would return.

Natalie made her famous red potato salad while Ma decided on an old family favorite for dessert. Once Joy arrived with Lindsey, Jackson got busy on grilling the steaks and the shrimp and veggie kabobs.

Ma convinced Boyd to wait until after dinner to surprise Lindsey with the ring, stretching Boyd's patience to the limit. His leg bounced through the meal even though it must have hurt to do so. Every time Lindsey looked at him he blushed and looked away, cluing her in to something going on. She asked him "What?" several times, but he would answer, "Nuthin'" and avert his eyes.

By the time the last morsel was eaten he seemed about ready to jump out of his skin. He waited for the plates to be cleared and Nana's special lemon crème cake to be put on the table and then he glanced at Ma, looking for her permission to pop the question.

She nodded. It was time.

"Lindsey," he began nervously. "I have a question to ask you." He pulled the small box from his pocket and placed it in front of her. "Go ahead. Look at it."

Lindsey looked around at all the expectant faces and then at the box. With one eyebrow raised in suspicion, she looked at them all again.

"No," she said.

Jackson could feel the air leave the room, sucked from deep within Boyd's anxiety filled chest.

"On your knees," she said to him and pointed to the floor.

Boyd sighed. He struggled, but managed to hold on to the table while attempting to kneel. The best he could do was resting his left knee on the floor while his right leg extended out in an awkward and seemingly painful position.

"Show me," Lindsey said, wanting him to open the box for her.

Jackson didn't think Boyd could possibly let go of his grip on the table, so he reached across and took the box, opening it in front of Lindsey.

"You want to marry me?" Boyd asked her.

Lindsey examined the ring and then looked at Boyd.

"Okay," she said with a shrug.

Everyone was able to breathe again.

The women clapped as Jackson helped his brother back into his seat. Lindsey surprised him and got up, put her hands on Boyd's shoulders in order to lean in and then kissed him. It was a short peck on the lips to seal the deal.

Jackson had never seen her show affection like that to Boyd. Boyd's face beamed like a headlamp in the darkness. Jackson supposed there was someone for everyone and he was happy his brother had found his someone.

"Congratulations, Buddy," he said, shaking Boyd's hand.

Boyd prodded him. "You have to find a ring for Natalie now."

"Who knows?" said Ma. "Maybe there will be a double wedding sometime in the future. Wouldn't that be fun?"

Jackson glanced over at Natalie and she grinned. They had already talked about a wedding, but decided it wouldn't happen before everyone was settled and, most important to Jackson, that Natalie's parents learned to trust him with their daughter's heart. There was no hurry. It was fun just getting to know one another again, crazy, cracks and all.

He winked and she returned the gesture.

Eternally. Yeah, he liked that idea too.

A NOTE FROM THE AUTHOR

On the night of January 26, 2013, I lost my beloved husband to suicide. Jim struggled his entire adult life with the deep-seeded demons only a cruel and abusive childhood could summon. For 45 years he fought the good fight, battling depression and addiction while trying his best to be a better husband and father than his role models ever were. In some ways he succeeded, while in other ways, he did not. In the end it all became too heavy a burden, with a narrowing opportunity to fix what he knew was wrong. In his last days, he saw no other alternative but to take his own life.

The story you have just read is not Jim's story, though elements of our experience as a family are sprinkled throughout. We are not alone in our circumstance. There are many families struggling to keep loved ones alive or grieving over a dear one's suicide. The struggle is real and exhausting for all involved. If you find yourself on any side of this crisis, please don't hesitate to find help. If someone says they are done with life, believe them, and be aware that you will not always be able to convince them otherwise. If you just want someone to talk to about your experiences, please reach out to another or feel free to contact me:

On Facebook at DonnaKnechtPatrick, or on

My website: www.donnaknechtpatrick@wordpress.com

I'd be honoured to hear from you and offer any help I can.

HELPFUL INFO

If you, or anyone you know are in crisis now, please do not hesitate to call the National Suicide Prevention Lifeline at:
1-800-273-TALK (8255)

To chat online with a counsellor:
http://www.suicidepreventionlifeline.org/GetHelp/LifelineChat.aspx

The National Suicide Prevention Lifeline website:
http://www.suicidepreventionlifeline.org/

For the hearing impaired, contact the Lifeline by TTY at:
1-800-799-4889

For those with intrusive thoughts, it turns out, you're not alone. Here is an enlightening link:
https://www.calmclinic.com/anxiety/symptoms/disturbing-thoughts

For those suffering with PTSD (trauma comes in many forms). Here are two helpful links:
http://www.ptsdalliance.org/
http://www.giftfromwithin.org/

www.ingramcontent.com/pod-product-compliance
Lightning Source LLC
Chambersburg PA
CBHW022111170626
46808CB00002B/689